MW00957672

Made from Raw Materials

A NOVEL

REV. FRANK E. BOURNER

ISBN 978-1-0980-4899-0 (paperback)
ISBN 978-1-0980-4900-3 (digital)

Copyright © 2020 by Rev. Frank E. Bourner

All rights reserved. No part of this publication may be reproduced, distributed, or transmitted in any form or by any means, including photocopying, recording, or other electronic or mechanical methods without the prior written permission of the publisher. For permission requests, solicit the publisher via the address below.

Christian Faith Publishing, Inc.
832 Park Avenue
Meadville, PA 16335
www.christianfaithpublishing.com

Printed in the United States of America

Preface

Why these fleeting moments? This is not the first time a *why* question has been asked. We have heard it in times of sickness and death. I personally ask this question not in time of trouble but in a year of reflection. I ask "Why am I here?" and "Why and how did I become the person I turned out to be?"

After considerable reflection, I concluded that life is given for each of us to discover God's purpose. I will never completely understand myself, but this one thing I know and try to communicate: I am more than I could have been if God and Christian community had not been a major influence. I borrow from Apostle Paul: "What I know is only partial, but someday face to face, I shall know even as now I am known" (1 Corinthians 13:12).

Deepest satisfaction came in quiet times with pen, paper, and reflective mind inviting me to visit friends separated by time and space. Some stepped forward quickly. Others came forward slowly and slipped quietly to my side. They whispered nearly forgotten experiences which once again allowed us to laugh, play, cry, hunt, fish, and work together for the kingdom Jesus taught. I am reminded of snares which trapped or I narrowly escaped. It is with hope that parts of this journey will help others avoid my faults and be better witnesses.

This is a story of my life from childhood to retirement. I am most grateful to God the Divine Potter (Isaiah 64:8), my wife of fifty-six years who served patiently beside me, and our two daughters who were instrumental for exciting youth meetings and mission trips. Christian friends must be credited. They patiently *tried* to train and guide me.

Acknowledgement

Many thanks to my good friends, June Lindimore and Mike Klein for their additional editing help.

Special thanks to Liz Donohue, artist, for her assistance in designing the cover art.

Artists see lovely possibilities in a slab of stone, a block of wood, or a flat canvas. A loving mother holds beautiful dreams for her newborn child. My mother did. She had the Presbyterian minister baptize her infant son. Astonishingly a person of significance was fashioned from and in his earthy frame. *Only* raw material? No! Actually, a person of significance is waiting in every human body to say hello to the world. The Divine Potter can make something beautiful and worthwhile out of a lump of clay.

Mother Earth

In early childhood, I enjoyed nature: mud, water, flowers, and trees. A favorite time was when Dad said, "Luke, get some buckets, a bushel basket, and a shovel. We are going to the mountains." Before midafternoon, we had them full of rich loam. He explained the mixture of sand, humus, and clay was perfect for planting flower and vegetable seeds. By spring, his self-built greenhouses were full of healthy tomato, pepper, marigold, petunia, and coleus plants for eager customers. I wanted to plant and even wait on customers. Dad said, "No! Maybe later. You can help by washing those clay pots or pull weeds."

Dad also formed rolls of moss to create funeral casket wreaths. Occasionally, I made mud balls in which Sis and I set dandelion, violet, and clover bloom stems. Sis loved gathering the small flowers from the field. In an hour or less, the flowers faded and died. Life and death was nothing. There was plenty more mud, blooms, and time. Death was not even a thought—until little Sis's dress caught on fire. Dad had built a blazing fire for us to roast marshmallows. He had even cut short twigs for each of us. The fire blazed. Sparks flew. We laughed. Children danced around until someone screamed: "Sis's dress is on fire!" Confusion followed. Dad rushed over. He rolled Sis over and over on the ground, picked her up, put her in the car, and sped off. That was the last I saw of Sis. I thought, *We will not pick flowers together again.*

Months later, Mom stayed in her room all day. Doctors came. Nancy told us to play quietly. Mom was taken away. Mom never came back. My little world stopped. Family life changed. I spent more time with Quack, Quack, my pet duck. One time after working in the garden, Dad helped me play with Quackie. He placed a tray of chicken mush and a bowl of beer about ten feet apart. We gathered around to watch Quackie go from one to the other until she became sleepy and laid down for a nap. Was Dad trying to lift our spirits?

Dad always worked hard. But now he worked still harder and longer and came home late. Nancy said he simply enjoyed drinking with his factory friends after work. One night, Dad brought a friend home to meet us: "I want you to call her Nani," he said. He had trouble for a moment with words and then mumbled, "Think of her as your new mom." Obviously, it did not set well with Jack and Nancy. Jack stomped the floor and ran out of the room. Nancy cried and turned away. Nani stretched her arms toward me. I responded. We hugged. Two days later, she presented me with a birthday cake and four candles.

Five tiny kittens showed up in our backyard one day. They were playful. Sister Nancy brought a pan of milk which they lapped up. Their whiskers draped with milk. The white one in my arms and close to my chest was a warm feeling. Jack came toward us with a burlap sack and a brick. Nancy spoke sharply, "Jack, what in the world are you doing?" He picked up one kitten at a time and put them in the sack. Nancy bellowed, "Jack! Stop!"

Jack promptly replied: "Dad said the cats had to go. He said, 'Take them back to the river where they came from. Nani does not like cats.'" From that day on, Nancy often referred to "Nani" as "Nasty."

When the Jingle Bike came down our street, Nani gave us each five cents for a Popsicle. On a few summer evenings, we would walk five blocks to Heiner's bakery for a loaf of freshly baked bread. Butter on warm bread was a joyous treat.

My spirits picked up when a new family moved into the house behind us. Their daughter was about my size. *A new friend to play with*, I thought. She was not fond of making mud balls and wreaths like Sis did. Girl stuff at her house was boring. One day our activity was interrupted with her mom's strange plan. She took our clothes off. She turned us around and around. She explained that it was to show Carol the difference. To me, it was senseless. It would have been forgotten if I had not told Nani.

The world exploded. She marched straight to Carol's house and shouted words I had only heard Dad use.

When Nani returned, she pointed her finger and spoke sternly, "Luke, stay away from Carol's house. Those people are bad."

"But Carol is my friend."

"Stay away. I mean it! Stop whimpering. Don't give me that ugly look and crying stuff. Go to your room. Now."

When sister Nancy came home, she sensed something was wrong. She came to my room. I told her what had happened. "Nancy, Nani said I can't visit my friend Carol anymore, never, never. I hurt all over. Mom is gone. Sis is gone, and now Carol. Nani is mean. I want to tell brother Jack. He will do something, maybe...Where is Jack? I never see him anymore."

"Luke, Nani said Jack simply packed his suitcase and left home to live with a school friend for a while. He will come back. I am here. I love you. Nani will calm down and change her mind. Let's be patient. We will try to please the best we can. Come here. Let's give each other a hug. We have each other."

Age six meant school. First grade was a breeze. Second grade teacher expected students to read. Normally, I could bow my head as if to hide and get skipped. Mrs. Tucker would still call my name. Fact was, I could not read two words. One afternoon after class, Mrs. Tucker told me to stay. "Luke, you are going to have to take second grade over next year. You just cannot read," she said. "Take this letter home to your parents."

The next day, Nani marched to the principal's office. Whatever happened there, no one knows, except I went to the third grade. After that, promotions were automatic.

Gym classes were a dread. There was one advantage of being slightly built; it was harder for the War Ball to find me. But when "Gorilla Jim" made me his target, it left a nice red spot. Also, that huge and heavy 20 lb. medicine ball was tough to catch. Actually, no one ever thought I would be an athlete or, as far as that goes, anything.

Life was full of humiliations. Preparing for school one morning, Nani bought me a pair of long-legged underwear to wear. "Put these on. The others are dirty."

"Nani, those are Jack's old undies. They are too long."

"Luke, you can't go to school with no underwear. You can wear them for one day."

"But they hang below my shorts. Everyone will see them and laugh at me. No, no."

"Okay, Luke, I will roll them up like this. Now they do not show. Get going, or you will be late."

For the first time, I wanted to call Nani the word Nancy often used: "Nani Nasty." Walking to school, they kept falling down. I repeatedly pushed them up and under. When the dismissal bell rang, I was relieved. Walking home, a buddy and I decided to call a couple kids a hundred or so yards behind that defamatory "N" word. They came after us. Running we could do, and that we did until breathlessly safe through my back door.

Relief came when Nani's sister Aunt Myrtle was given permission to take me for a few days. It was likely a reprieve for Nani. Nancy hastily clued me about Myrtle: "She is considered *black sheep* of the seven sisters. She is a beautician. She is an alcoholic. She misses work a lot. She has a part-time car-racing live-in friend, Tracy. He drops by to stay with her once in a while."

I thought, *She could not be as harsh as Nani Nasty*. Myrtle took me on my first Greyhound trip. We went to Dayton, Ohio, to meet him. He showed me pictures of his Hudson race car and many trophies.

Once we were back in Huntington, Aunt Myrtle announced, "Luke, we are going to shop for some new clothes for you. Stores are close by. The shorts, sweater, brogans, and knee-high socks looked expensive. Go and try them on." When I came out of the small room, she had a big smile. "We will take them," she said and pulled out a wad of money from under her shirt.

"Thank you, Aunt Myrtle. You are always trying to help me."

Then Auntie said, "Let us go over to Jim's spaghetti's restaurant and get a good dinner. Like that?"

"Yes, ma'am!"

Nani had six sisters. One evening after dinner of squirrel, gravy, biscuits, and green beans, Nani announced, "Tomorrow morning, we are going to Sister Nel's church homecoming and picnic." Going to the country was always a pleasant experience (well, except for church and the flies). Thank goodness the church was packed to overflow. I gladly stayed outside. Dad hung around a car where friends passed his bottle around. After the preacher bellowed something about heaven and hell, the people sang and filed out of the small white church. The best part followed. Tables were loaded with all kinds of country food. A couple women waved cardboard fans to keep flies away for a moment with little effect. They simply flew to sample another dish. Horseshoes were heard clanging somewhere behind the church.

Nel's humble house sat upon an elevated grade above the dirt road. That evening, I joined the family on the porch where they chatted about cousins, number of hogs killed last winter, fox that got the chickens, and on and on. When a car drove by, we waved. Dad must have sensed my boredom.

"Luke, would you like me to show you how to make an airplane?"

"An airplane?"

"Yes, I'll show you." He stepped off the porch, gathered up half-used cigarettes, and slowly emptied the tobacco.

"I thought you were going to make a plane?"

"Hold on, Son!" Curiosity held my attention. Then Dad, with a cupped right hand, caught one of the countless flies. Then he began to demonstrate. He twisted a tiny piece of cigarette paper into a point, spread the opposite end into a tiny fan that served as a wing, stuck the pointed end into thc rump of the winged insect, and let her loose. She flew up, up, around, around, and around.

After a few experiments, I had made my own arsenal of planes. My other favorite activity was down at the small creek nearby. When Dad saw me looking in that direction, he said, "Not today. We have no hooks." After that, I made sure we were supplied with proper equipment. Worms were easy to find. Half-rotten manure behind the barn supplied plenty of tiny wiggling red worms. The fish we caught were bluegills, suckers, and six-by-eight inches catfish. I enjoyed throwing them back in the water.

When supper was ready, I hovered close to the cast-iron kitchen stove with a purpose in mind: *Get to the food before the flies do.* Someone would sense my concern and hand me a biscuit or a chicken leg. Children's drink of the day was fresh cow's milk. Yuck. I had no interest.

The next day, I told friends of my country visit and especially the Barnum and Bailey Circus act. When cousin Paul had to go do his business, he took me to a deep nearby gully. It must have been eighteen feet deep. I sheepishly stayed back. He slipped down his pants, walked out on a log, squatted, and you know what? A circus crowd would have applauded. I did.

By next spring, Dad had rented a new house and reconstructed his two greenhouses. I fell in love with our new place mainly because of the large two adjoining lots. The front had boulders, fish pond, and large trees. A chest-high stone wall dividing the lots made a perfect setting to play cowboys and robbers. With my stack of comic books, I learned about the role of my heroes: Superman, Lone Ranger, Gene Autry, and the Green Hornet. A large piece of green felt in the attic draping over my back made my role of Green Hornet authentic. My two new cap pistols with live caps made me a real cowboy.

A family across the dirt alley had four boys. The brothers in age were Josh, Robbie, Earl, and Dale. One day the red-headed one waved. I returned the gesture. Without hesitation, he came over. It became the beginning of a lasting friendship. Robbie was about my height but stouter. His brothers called him "Pit Bull." Since he came to like me, the friendship was welcomed. Robbie's hair was flashing red. His freckles were as prominent as his hair. Only once did a neighborhood kid dare call him "Freckle Face." It didn't take long to join in games of mud-lot basketball, softball, kick the can, and marbles. Life became enjoyable.

One day while Dad was busy planting sweet potato slices in a cold frame, he turned and asked, "What are you boys doing in that pile of scrap wood?"

"Well, Robbie and I want to make a rubber gun like Uncle Pete told us about. Would you have time to help us? We need a small board like you use to make seed flats and a small piece of rubber."

Dad seemed to know exactly what I was talking about. He stopped planting and walked into the old shed. Robbie, with a degree of surprise, turned to me and said, "Your dad's good. He's taking time to help us." I made the same observation. I thought to myself, *Maybe Dad wants our company.* In a couple minutes, Dad came out of the shed with the perfect board and an old tire inner tube. "Wow!"

Within half an hour, two guns were made. With that rubber, wood, and a bit of engineering, we were ready. We could hit our target twenty feet away or (if we desired) another person. It stung a bit, but one could say to his opponent without dispute, "You're dead!"

Dad said, "Boys, be careful. Shoot at cans or trees, but don't shoot at each other. That clear?"

"Yes, Dad."

Rubber gun games didn't last long until we decided to use the old inner tube rubber to make slingshots. With a choice forked stick, rubber strips, and a leather shoe tongue, we had a more lethal weapon. We shot at tin cans, trees, or whatever but no windows.

A group of boys from somewhere over the railroad tracks also had weapons. Occasionally, we taunted each other. Later, we shot a few pebbles. Unfortunately, the game of taunt and fun became serious. Dale said, "We are going to win this battle."

Dale thought of himself as a leader, and we usually followed. Maybe we followed because he was older and simply took charge. Dale found a large tree branch fork, nailed it to the old Sycamore tree trunk, and with the wider rubber strips, we let the baseball-sized rock fly from behind our stone wall. Fly it did across the street into front yards. Thank goodness no car or person was hit. But one of their small pebbles did. In the midst of the fury, one of the enemies' irregular pebbles zigzagged through the air toward me. Standing upright like a brave leader with my fist in the air, that pebble made a zigzag into my forehead. Pretending it missed, I casually wiped a trickle of blood away and responded: "Hey, you dumb heads, why don't you learn to shoot?" Slowly but surely, I came to realize our battle activity was dangerous. Little Josh turned for home. I realized it was time to find another activity and suggested a game of basketball. Dale responded, "It is too muddy over there." Nani stepped out the screen door and called, "Dinner's ready." The others left.

After supper, Dad handed me a package wrapped in brown paper and said, "This is for your birthday."

"What in the world could it be. A BB gun maybe," I said.

"No, Son. It is a .22 riffle." As I fumbled with the package, Dad went on with a lecture, "This gift is not a play toy. It is a single shot. You put in one shell at a time and then reload. This gun can be dangerous. I will keep it until we go to the country and practice."

The next Saturday, we drove forty miles to Uncle Pete's and Aunt Annie's spacious farm. After all that "Hello, how are you?

Glad you came" stuff, the guys gathered together in the front yard. Cousin Lonnie planted a nickel on a post about forty feet away. Each took a shot. They missed. Dad didn't. I noticed that each time he prepared to shoot, he spit on his finger and wiped the small rifle sights. I couldn't wait until next Saturday when we would go rabbit hunting. Anxious to try my skills, I was given privilege to go to the river next week and practice. The Ohio was out of its banks. What a surprise. Rats were forced out of their holes. Some were in a trash pile until I kicked it. What a good day to target practice. Some of those varmints leapt into the muddy water and swam "bang, bang" for a moment. Wow! Encouraging thoughts flashed through my mind, *I'm getting good at this. Dad will be proud of me. Maybe he will go with me to the river sometime even with the men rabbit hunting.* My body surged with excitement as I hurried home.

When Dad came home from the factory, I quickly explained my target practice.

He said, "Proud of you, Son, really proud. But now I have a few jobs around here for you this week. See that stack of flower pots and wash tub? Wash dirt off flower pots. And after that, sift that load of dirt in the backyard."

"Dad!"

"Just do it. Or would you rather pull weeds?"

Next morning, washing old dirty pots was grimy. I left the pots and tried sifting dirt. After a few shovels of dirt in the wire screen and a shake or two, I simply gave up. When my buddies called for me to play horseshoes in their yard, I ran. Robbie and I were partners. Robbie threw his first shoe short of the peg, and I quickly shouted: "Throw the next shoe to knock it up."

Maryland, Dale's girlfriend, quickly responded: "How do you knock up a horseshoe?" The guys laughed. I was puzzled. What was so funny?

About noon, Nani screamed to my embarrassment, "Luke Leon Gray, come home!" When she used my middle name, she meant *now*.

She met me at the door with firm words, "Where have you been? I know exactly where you spent the day!"

"You really think you know?"

"Yes, I do. I can tell by the mud you carry home on your shoes."

"Your dad will expect your jobs to be completed."

Actually, when he arrived, he said nothing about my tasks. He had something else in mind.

"Tomorrow morning, we are going to fish."

"Where?"

"'Four Pole Creek where we went the last time. It is shallow enough for you to wade."

"Dad, I can swim now. Cousin Lonnie taught me to dog paddle last summer." Dad smiled in disbelief.

By 9:00 a.m., we were in the water. The creek of Dad's choice was not more than chin deep (my chin, that is). My welcomed task was to dig mud eels out of black foul-looking slime. When they came squirming out, I grabbed and threw them in my bucket. With excellent bait, we caught fish for dinner.

On warm summer evenings, we camped on Mud River. Nancy had other interests; she excused herself. Nani, Uncle Everett, and Aunt Eve joined us by a fire. Dad and Everett set a trotline. They used crawfish or minnows for bait. Some catfish we caught were almost too big to fit in a wash tub. Men in the factory named Dad "Catfish" which he was proud of. When dark, we waded in waist-deep water to gig bullfrogs. With a flashlight shining in their eyes, they were easy to catch by hand. The gig was occasionally used to steer snakes away. Later in the night, they checked the lines. Nani and Eve began packing our gear.

"What are you doing? I asked.

"We need to start home soon."

"Dad, why can't we just spend the night here?"

"No, Everett must work tomorrow, and there are fish and frogs to clean. Tomorrow morning, we will come back and take up the lines."

Once at home and comfortably in bed, I had trouble sleeping. The good experiences swirled around in my head: warm water up to my chin, crawfish under a rock, catfish, frogs and the campfire. The logs crackled, popped, and sent sparks into the air. I counted burning ash floating upward one after another after another. The fire slowly faded until the bed shook.

Dad said, "Luke, it is nine thirty. You plan to go with me to the river?" We caught more fish to take home.

That afternoon when the sun was blazing hot, Robbie came running over, "We are going to the river for a swim. You want to join us?"

"Sure. Yes, yes! Let me get my bathing suit."

"You don't need it. Come on. Dale and the guys are waiting. Come on!"

It was not far to the river. We crossed through Robbie's yard past the basketball lot, a neighbor's yard, over the steep earthen flood wall, and through the scratching cornfield to their favorite swimming spot. One by one, clothes came off. The brothers lined up like stair steps in height. They strutted back-and-forth on the beach. Each followed the other until all had displayed their wares and capabilities. Then they jumped in the water, splashed, and laughed. *What a strange exercise*, I thought.

"Josh, what were they doing?" I causally asked.

"It's just something they like. We are a little young. Someday, you will understand. Take off your clothes."(I did, slowly.) As I slithered into the water, each ripple bounced around my head as if questioning, "Someday, you will understand."

Understand what? Am I missing something important? Those words came flooding back. Yes, when I vacationed at Uncle Pete's Farm. I joined cousins Homer and Lonnie on a two-mile railroad hike to a country store. We each bought a pint of ice cream, played the gumball machine for a prize, and started our trek back. Lonnie and Homer fumbled pages in what they called a girlie book. I asked to look. They said, "Not now, someday." I was left out of a secret again. While mulling over the rebuke, Dale said, "Listen, I have a test for you all. Pick up a rock to hold your feet on the bottom of the river and see who can walk the greatest distance. I will go first." Each followed. I was last. To my disbelief and to their amazement, I won.

One day after our swim, Dale sprang another one of his crazy ideas, "Let's cross the river."

Earl quickly replied, "Tell me how? It is too wide to swim. It must me one mile. There are coal barges out there."

Dale had the answer, "We will make a raft! There is plenty of drift wood and logs along the shore. Come on. Get going. We can do it!"

Soon, we were on our way naked and all. Dale kick paddled from the back. Rest of us used our arms or a small piece of wood to stroke from the side.

Exhausted but safe on the Ohio shore, we slumped on the sand long enough to realize what we had done.

Dale, realizing our situation, said, "Hey, guys, we have drifted a long way down river. We better start back now."

One hour later, we were safe on the WV side, but to our surprise, we were below Twelve Pole Creek. It looked more like a river. "There must have been a storm up stream," Dale remarked. "Rushing water, logs, trash, cans, plastic jugs could push us right back into the Ohio River." Dale continued, "We have few options. We can't go straight ahead. You hear the traffic on the four-lane highway? On the other side, you can see and hear that amusement park. Picnic tables are in clear sight. Guys, we have no choice. We must swim the flooded stream. There is no other way."

An awakening pause followed. Finally, Dale said with a sense of finality, "I will go first. Once on the other side, send Josh." Dale made it with ease. He motioned so as not to attract people at the park (come on). It was Josh's turn, but he froze. We coached. He quivered. We begged to no avail. It became a pressure situation. Robbie and Earl simply grabbed Josh and threw him in. Finally, all of us were over where we needed to be. We hid behind trees. Then one by one, we sprinted like foreign soldiers from tree to tree. After a long walk, we found our clothes where we left them.

After a few weeks, I asked, "Dad, can we go fishing Saturday?"

"No. The water has turned colder. Fish don't bite as well. We will put fishing off till spring. I will take you squirrel hunting when season comes in. That okay? Besides, bowling leagues begin soon. I will be out three nights a week. I plan for you and Nani to go with me."

"Oh, no," I groaned. "There is nothing for me to do there. The smoke is thick."

"Well, I tell you what. We will drop you off at the theater. That okay?"

"That will be great. I may be able to watch *Lone Ranger* and *Tarzan*."

On the first day of squirrel season, we were parked along a lonely road far into the country. Dad had his .12 gage double-barrel shotgun, and I had my .22 single barrel.

"Dad," I said, "it is dark. We won't see anything."

He replied, "Son, we wait until dawn. The idea is to find a place in the woods before squirrels' start to move."

About daylight, I took a seat by a large tree and waited; it seemed forever. The squirrel came walking across tree limbs, jumped to a large tree, and paused. I wet the sights, aimed, and fired. That was my first kill, except for the river rats. When Dad and I met, he said, "See any?"

"Yes, and I killed it with my .22. I mean my BB gun." He smiled. On the way, home. I asked, "Dad, can we go again next Saturday?"

"Most likely."

"Great." Hunting occupied my mind morning and night. I could see the squirrel tails dangling from the car antenna like my country cousins displayed theirs. It would be a sign of my accomplishments. Maybe someday I could be a hunting or even fishing guide like Dad's magazine advertises. I could lead people over hills, out of deep valleys, or find fish bait and good fish spots. Although Dad would like me to take over the flower and vegetable business, he would be pleased if I made sporting my vocation. That will never happen as my tired mind drifted off into wonderland.

Next week, Dad came home with a dog. With excitement, I asked, "Is he a squirrel dog?"

"No, she is a Blue Tick Coon dog. Her name is Blue. Everett and I bought it together. We plan to try it out this weekend."

"I can go?"

"Yes, but it will be at night. There will be a lot of walking. We will stay out far past your bedtime."

"Dad, you know I can do it."

"Okay. From now on, you have a job. You must feed Blue and water her every day!"

"That will be fun. She will be my friend."

The next Friday, we started out near Everett's house. The hills were steep and valleys deep. After about an hour, Old Blue let out a whimper and then a continued howl.

Everett said, "She is on a hot trail. We better keep up. Come on. Never know how far she will go before she trees." We must have huffed and buffed two miles up and down and wormed through thickets until we found Blue barking up a large oak tree. Dad shined his five-cell flashlight in the Coon's eyes, took his riffle (my .22, that is), and fired. The animal hit the ground, snarling. A fierce fight erupted. Old Blue won. Dad put the Coon in his hunting jacket.

"What are you going to do with it?" I asked.

"I will show you later." That night, three Opossums were treed.

Next morning, I watched as Dad took his hunting knife and began cutting fur from the Coon's body. Somewhat puzzled, I inquired, "What's your plan?"

"Luke, this fur will sell for a couple dollars at Tony's Trading Post. The Opossum skins are worth about seventy-five cents. You can have the money for yourself." The skins were pulled over hand crafted wood boards and nailed to our garage door. It took on a unique character.

Occasionally, to our regret, Blue would drag in a Polecat. Dad or Everett came prepared. They always carried along a paper flour bag in which they dropped the smelling animal. With the flour sack tightly bound, the pungent odor was mostly contained. Everett exclaimed, "You can't skin that thing."

Dad quickly responded, "Everett, we will bury it in the ground for a couple weeks, and the odor will leave. It's simple."

A week later, more fur was added to our door collection. My cousins taught me another adventurous game collection skill. They gave me two steel traps and showed me how to use them. I waded small creeks and placed the traps at muskrat slides and den openings. Their skins were valuable. When I asked Dad why I often had a foot in the trap but no muskrat, he explained, "A muskrat will chew it's ankle off to free it's self from the trap. It loses a foot but saves its life."

"It treasures life more than a limb," I reflected. A chill crept up my spine as if it was my own foot.

Dad went on to coach, "Luke, next time place the traps near deep water. The weight of the trap will drown your catch. Got it, Son?"

That year, our furs were sold for $57 dollars. With that much cash in my hand, I began thinking of a new gun to buy. Daily life was a constant rush. Dad worked constantly. I asked, "Dad, why do you work so hard and almost all the time?"

His answer came quickly and harsh. "Our house is not paid for. I have to pay the bank every month. Besides, we have to eat. We like to hunt and fish. I plan to bowl. And then you talk a lot about a new gun, don't you? You see. It takes work."

"Okay, I get it," I sheepishly answered.

It pleased me to hear him voice my desire for a more powerful gun. I knew Dad wanted me to hunt with him; he never said it, but I could tell. After his factory labor, he had a quick dinner, and then he was off to the greenhouses or building a new cold frame. Three nights, he was off to the bowling lanes. Well, I was busy too. There was school. Dad pulled strings. He said he'd get me into East Trade School which was a forty-minute bus ride across town. School was easy. English and history classes required no tests. Math was easy for me. The trade classes were enjoyable.

My new gold school sweater seemed to catch a neighbor girl's eye. It took a while before her brother Rich invited me over to meet his family: his mother, aunt, and, of course, Sally. They seemed to enjoy inviting me over. We played parcheesi, dominos, rummy, and after dark, Kick the Can. One night, Sally called for a game of hide-and-seek. Belinda (Rich's girlfriend) added that Aunt Gerry would be the hunter. Okay, let's go.

Sally took my hand and said, "Come with me. I know some good hiding places." It was the crawl space under an old shed with spiderwebs. She held me close, squeezed my hand.

That was when I noticed that something strange began happening to my lower body. It was a tingle or something really different. It was definitely awkward. I asked, "Sally, let's get out of this rat-infested place." I nudged her out. I did not care to play that game again. Sally was interesting, but girls just don't enjoy what my buddies and I like to do. My heart was predominately occupied with hunting and river activities. That would never change! Or would it? Could it? Never.

Those days when I had wished for a gun like Dad's finally came. Tuesday before our Thanksgiving visit to my sister's home on the beautiful Coan River in Virginia, Dad handed me a full choke .20-guage shotgun. What a beauty.

"Dad, Dad, how can I thank you?" I exclaimed. He smiled. Then I did something strange. It was completely foreign to me. I ran over and literally gave Dad a big bear hug. An awkward silence followed. Both of us seemed embarrassed for a moment.

Quickly, Dad began showing the gun's operation. He presented cleaning materials and said, "Take care of it, Son. It can last for the rest of your life." I was still beaming when he left for the garden.

Steve and I were up before daylight on Thanksgiving morning. One voice came from the bedroom, "Be back on time for dinner!"

"We will," Steve replied.

Three duck decoys were thrown over the twenty feet embankment into Coan River. About daylight, two mallards flew in. We took the johnboat to pick them up and crossed to the other shore to place more decoys. Hidden behind brush, we waited. The sun was casting shadows when a flock swooped in for a landing. We stood and fired away. It must have sounded like a warzone. They flew away. Only our decoys remained.

"Steve, what now?" I asked.

"Luke, I want to show you something you have never done before. The decoys can wait. We are going to walk the shoreline for arrowheads." We walked and scanned the sand and rocks. In a few minutes, he bent over, picked up a rock, and studied it.

"What kind of rock is it? Tell me."

"This is not just a rock." Holding it before me, he added, "This is an Indian arrowhead." He paused. He stared and studied like it might be an ancient gold coin. "Luke," he continued, "this arrow point is thousands of years old. The Indian who lost it once stood right where we now stand. He held this point. Take it. Now you hold it. This is how close we are to that early hunter. It is yours."

"Thanks, thanks very much."

We walked on and on. Steve picked up a broken piece of glass and began looking around. He looked up a steep clay bank and pointed. "Let's go up and look in that dilapidated shack. Follow me."

Under the fallen timbers, he picked up a bottle.

"What is it, Steve?"

"This is an old whiskey bottle. Old timers used to make home brew around here. Keep looking. We might find more." We filled a grain sack nearly full and walked back to the shore.

On our way back to where we left the boat, two ducks scurried from the brush. Steve shot the first one. The other one waddled toward water. Steve ran and threw his arms wide and body over the fleeing bird. He caught it alive. We laughed to the point of giggles. Still laughing and walking, I continued hunting arrowheads.

Steve called, "Not that way. We better start back. We have walked a long way from our boat. The other direction, Luke."

As we walked, I felt a need to share a little of my daily life and appreciation. "Steve, you have opened my mind to new possibilities. I live near the Ohio River. We have many ducks. I could even search the shoreline for Indian signs, except…well, I have no boat. So…well, except I have no boat."

"Luke, I may have an answer for you. We have a couple rubber rafts in the boathouse. You can have one of them. It would need pumped up. Pop has numerous boats of all sizes, a couple john boats, cruise boat for pleasure, and several for fishing and oyster planting. People around here call Pop "Popeye." He will gladly take you fishing sometime. The raft will allow you set decoys and retrieve them."

"Steve, thank you for the offer. Maybe you could come down and hunt with me sometime?"

"Luke, I would love to, but I am on the junior basketball team this year. Besides, Pop expects be to work around here when he can catch me. You know what I mean? Pop is kind and seems to understand. Whenever I make a mistake, which I have often done, he normally looks me in the eye and says, 'Son, did you learn anything?' That is pretty much my life. What about your days at home?"

"Well, Steve, Dad doesn't talk much. He stays busy. I sift dirt, pull weeds, and try to slip away when I can. It does not seem to bother Dad much. At least he does not show it. He never scolds me. I do carry boxes of flowers to the car for customers. Nani watches a lot of TV, prepares meals, and transplants seedlings in the greenhouse.

"Dad and I enjoy fishing and hunting together. For a short time, I worked for a local store. My main job was to deliver groceries on my bicycle until complaints about broken eggs. Billy Joe and I walked the halls at school. We hoped to catch a girl's attention, but it did not work. My joy has always been to get with buddies for games or swimming at the river. Life is pretty simple."

Steve seemed to appreciate my sharing. Then he pointed and said, "Look, we are back to our boat. Let us gather up the decoys and paddle back to the house. We should be there in time for Thanksgiving dinner. What a morning we have had."

"Yes, and the live mallard in your arms is beautiful. It reminds me of the pet duck I had as a little boy. Why don't we turn it free?" I asked.

Steve sensed my feelings. He slowly responded, "I may turn it loose in our farm pond."

The days ahead looked especially bright. Images of finding arrowheads, old bottles, and setting duck decoys with my new rubber raft twirled around in my head. Life looked good.

When Dad caught me alone, he warned, "The raft you are excited about can be dangerous. You turn it over, and you will lose your new gun. You could lose your life in the cold swift river. It could be the end, Luke, the very end. You must be careful. Do you hear me!"

"Yes, yes, Dad. I am always careful. When I go to the Ohio, I will stay close to the shore."

Trade school kept me busy. The program required six weeks of woodwork followed by sheet metal, welding, and electricity.

I planned to make electricity my third-year major. Maybe it would become my lifetime work.

On Saturday, I was off in high spirits to the river with raft, small paddle, shotgun, and two decoys. Dad cautioned me again. The river was swift and high to the tree line. I was able to get the decoys out about ten feet, enough for a flight of ducks to see them. Weights held the decoys in place. They wobbled and moved back-and-forth. I hid myself half way up the high bank and waited patiently—until shotguns began blasting from over my head. Tree branches splintered. One decoy bounced a foot in the air and fell on its side. The mallard's head was blown away. I screamed, "Stop! Stop! I am down here. Stop."

A moment of silence followed. The shooters said, "Sorry, sorry. We will pay you for the decoys." I slowly climbed up to meet them. They continued to apologize and pay. "No need to pay. They were given to me. Forget it."

They continued, "We are from Ironton, Kentucky. We are rabbit hunting with one eye open for ducks. We heard your duck call. Your decoys fooled us. You want to join us rabbit hunting?"

"Thanks, yes, would love to."

We had walked about a quarter of a mile when several ducks flew and lit in the river nearby. We froze. Three guns fired away. They flew, except one. I shouted, "We got one. No, I believe it is wounded. Here, hold my gun. I will take my raft and retrieve it." I carefully slid the raft in the water and began to paddle toward the wounded game. When about three feet from the duck, I lifted my paddle and gave a hard slap. The creature dove, disappeared, and came up ten feet further away. My repeated paddling and slapping was nonproductive. I suddenly realized darkness was upon me. I had floated far from my new friends and paddled to shore. Wet and discouraged, I left the raft and started my hike toward car headlights on the highway half a mile away. Walking home was my priority.

A car pulled over and stopped in front of me. Dad got out his car and began to question when another car joined us. The two hunting friends handed me my gun. Together, we tried to explain our experience. I gave them my name and phone number. We agreed to get together for a hunt in Kentucky. Dad and I traveled home together in silence.

Winter and spring flew by like a warm breeze. There were more hunting outings with old pals, Dad, and cousins. I linked with Robbie's brothers fishing in the Ohio. Our successful strategy for Catfish was to catch a large grasshopper and put it on the hook. Also, a hook wrapped with tinfoil produced skipjacks below the large county sewer drain. We didn't think about the filth that poured out. We could swim a quarter mile below where the water was clear of the ugly stuff.

School was okay. Electric shop grades were excellent. Driver education classes helped convince Dad that I was ready to drive. Now I could deliver flower orders to customers.

It was a hot, humid summer day when I asked Sally to join me for a swim in the river. Dad and Nani were not home. Sally's Aunt and mother insisted on joining us. They brought a blanket for sunbathing. They could not swim nor could Sally, but I could. The water was warm. I took Sally's hand and led her into the water, ankle deep, and waist deep—deeper until she could not touch the bottom. I welcomed her arms tightly around me. It was enjoyable until my toes sent an alarming message, "You are at the edge of a drop off. The sand under your feet is moving the wrong way." The next step was water of ten feet over our heads. I appealed for Sally to turn loose. She clung tighter. We went down and sprang up, down, and up until I broke her loose and pushed her toward the bank. This was repeated until we eventually reached the shore exhausted. Auntie and Mom had not moved. They were paralyzed. After collecting ourselves, we quietly trudged toward home.

A couple nights later, Sally and I took a stroll to Camden amusement park. We sat on a bench in a quiet corner. Sally broke the long silence, "Luke, you have not said a word. What are you thinking?" Silence continued. Finally I said words I had never thought or spoken, "I…I…I am thinking, thinking… about God."

In a couple moments, Sally suggested something that would eventually change my life. "Why don't you go to church with me Sunday?"

"Sally, I am not sure. Maybe, well, I will consider it."

As we walked slowly toward home, Sally kept talking. I heard not a word she said. My mind was on that word: God. *Where did it come from? Does the Almighty speak through people's heads, though near tragedy, through another person like Sally? I almost died. I am alive now. God, life, they seem to go together*, I thought.

The next morning, I managed to ask, "Nani, Sally asked me to attend church with her next Sunday. What do you think?"

She replied, "Do you want to go?"

"Yes, Nani."

"Why would you want to waste a morning in church? There may be other things your Dad would want us to do."

"Sally really wants me to go."

The next week, Sally's mother, Marie, visited with the same invitation. Nani asked, "Marie, what church are you talking about? Where is it?"

"Nani, we go to the Methodist Church just up the street."

"I appreciate your interest, but Marie, my answer is no. Besides, Luke does not have clothes fit for that big church. Some weekends, we camp and fish. Luke enjoys it a lot."

"Okay. Think about it. We would love to have him and you also. I will check back with you again sometime."

Marie must have spoken to her minister. Days later, he came knocking at the door. He made his acquaintance and invited the family to church. Persistently, he visited two more times. On the third visit, he said, "Mrs. Gray, is Luke home?"

"No, he is somewhere in the neighborhood. Don't know where exactly."

"Mrs. Gray, our youth at the church are going to attend a youth congress and would like for Luke to come with us. It is a week-long. I will be a lot of fun. I will be driving and will bring them back. Would you like for him to be a part of this wonderful activity? Everyone will be casual, jeans, and tee shirts. The cost is $32, and the church pays half of it. He would only need $16. You like the idea?"

"Well, maybe. His dad likes to take Luke fishing on weekends. He also has work for him to do. I will talk with Luke and his dad. It might work. We'll see. Thank you."

Rev. Shepherd told crazy jokes as we drove through the W. Va. Mountains to West Virginia Wesleyan College. We laughed. Four were roomed together. Each had his own bunk bed. The first evening activity was strange but interesting. One person read from a book they called the Bible. Each bowed his head. Later, they told me it was their way of talking to God.

On the last day before going home, we gathered on the lawn in a large circle, held hands, and sang songs like "Kumbaya" and "Into My Heart, Lord Jesus." Each person was given a candle. The one beside me lit mine, and I turned to the girl beside me and lit hers. Individuals spoke prayers. The warm feeling inside moved me to say something, but words would not come out. A strange and different feeling stirred within me. Something entirely new was happening, and it was good.

Before we arrived home, Rev. Shepherd said, "I will see you all in church tomorrow and again at youth meeting Sunday night. Sally responded, "We will be there."

Now more than ever, church attending became compelling. My mind was made up. When the opportunity was available my voice spoke with a certain degree of certainty, "Nani, I am going to church this Sunday with Sally."

"Okay, Luke, if you insist. When your dad is paid, we will go shopping for some church kind of clothes, maybe this Saturday."

The city bus let us out on Main Street. The suit she picked had sleeves down to my fingertips. The trousers nearly dragged the floor. The clerk suggested a smaller size. Nani said, "Luke is growing fast. He will grow into this one. We will take it!"

"Luke, you will grow into it before you know it." Nani picked out a tie and tied it on. "Nani, the thing feels awful." The mirror she pushed me toward spoke back at me. "You look weird."

An elderly stoutly built man met us at the church door with a warm greeting. His large hands and wide smile sat my racing heart at ease. After the service, Sally asked my opinion.

"Sally, it was interesting but dull. Youth Congress was much more enjoyable."

Sally responded quickly, "Oh, you need to visit our youth program. We meet every Sunday evening. It is more like our experience at youth congress. There are games like Musical Chairs, Jacob and Rachel. We sing rounds like 'John, Jacob, Jingle Heimer Schmidt' and 'Stand the Storm It Will Not Be Long.' The minister usually reads from the Bible and talks."

Wednesday evening prayer service was different but enjoyable. The people were much older, except for Babs who was a couple years younger than me. She played the piano. She was super nice, had a big smile, and warmly greeted me before and after the services. We sang songs like "What a Friend We Have in Jesus," "Leaning on the Everlasting Arms," "Blessed Assurance," "Whispering Hope," and the one I asked for every Wednesday, "I Found a Friend, Oh, Such a Friend."

Babs joined me for a youth hayride outing. The two of us, Jim, and his girlfriend just happened to sink deep into the hay likely longer than we should have stayed hidden. Unfortunately, that evening, Dr. Wright was assigned to chaperone. He had recently been assigned to the staff as visiting pastor. After the evening ride, Dr. Wright pointed to the hay lovers and told us to meet in his office. He scolded us for our terrible behavior. "You are supposed to set a good example. Boys, never display that vulgar behavior again. You hear me!"

"Yes, sir. Yes, sir. We will do better from now on. We promise." As we walked down the hall, we smiled at each other and giggled lightly.

Babs often invited me to stay after prayer services and sing more songs. Occasionally, we went to her home to talk about the church. Her parents welcomed me with open arms. One evening, I asked, "Babs, when I can get our car, would you go for an evening drive with me?"

"Yes, Luke, I would love it." Ohio River swimming paled in comparison to this new adventure.

On a Saturday evening, we went to Huntington Rose Garden. The spraying water pond, gold fish, and flowers were romantic. We held hands as we walked around until we came to a large oak tree. We rubbed faces which followed with a kiss and more and more kisses until nearly dark. The sensation which was felt when Sally held my hand under her old shed was mild compared to this new feeling. I wanted to stay in the Rose Garden longer, but we promised Bab's parents to return home before dark.

That night, there was a pain in my groin. The next morning, I knew I had to call our family doctor. Dr. Walkins asked me questions about my activities, "Been working in the garden? Playing ball? Swimming?" Then I told him about last night.

Dr. Watkins said, "Son, you will be all right in a few hours. Soak in your bathtub for at least a half hour. I promise you will feel better." Why Dr. Watkins bothered to call Nani. I do not know. When Nani asked me why I called Dr. Watkins, I tried to explain, "Dr. Watkins said I probably pulled a muscle playing basketball." Nani smiled.

Being elected as president to the youth group was later followed by appointment as president of the Tri-County Youth Association. My river pals did not understand my compulsion for church activities. They rejected invitations to join my new adventures. "You will enjoy the activities," I insisted. Later when they crossed the street to the other side, I wondered if it was my imagination, or were they deliberately avoiding me?

Time was flying by faster than the roller coaster at Camden Park. Before one event was over, plans were formulating for the next event. Squirrel season came upon me ever too quickly. When Dad said, "As a matter of fact, we will go Squirrel hunting this Saturday," I froze in my tracks physically and emotionally.

"Oh, Dad," I muttered. "That is the weekend of our district retreat."

Dad quickly retorted, "You can't do that. We always hunt together on the first day."

"But, Dad, I have no choice. I present the speakers. There are numerous responsibilities. Maybe next Saturday. Let's plan for next Saturday? Okay?"

Dad frowned. With slumped shoulders, he slowly walked away. Dad was hurt. I felt it. He was hurt deeply. I felt bad. I almost thought out loud, *Has something taken my love for hunting and fishing away? My new interests hurt Dad.*

High school was uneventful. A degree in electricity started my search for a job. Needing income to accomplish personal goals prompted an acceptance as stock clerk at Sylvania. My big private dreams pressed me on.

First I would purchase a car. Second would be a small house of my own. It would have a small pond nearby to stock fish and frogs. Thirdly there will be a little woman to live in the little home, maybe one like Babs. I could do it. Nothing could prevent it. A couple words recalled from the high school graduation speech came to mind: "Be careful what you dream for. Your dream may come true." On reflection, it sounded hopeful. On second thought, it sounded like a threat. I remained hopeful.

Jennings was coworker in the stockroom. Jennings was very religious. Throughout the days ahead, he questioned my faith,

"Are you a Christian? How do you know? Have you been baptized? Been immersed? Do you go to church? What church?" My answers did not seem to satisfy him.

He questioned, "Will you come with me tonight for a youth gathering? It will be at my house." Reluctantly, I accepted.

There were fifteen youth crowded in his small living room. Some sat on the floor. Jennings read from his King James Bible: "If you confess with your mouth that that Jesus is Lord and believe with your heart that God raised Him from the dead, you will be saved" (Romans 10:9). Then he looked at Mary, one of the younger of the group, and asked, "Mary, have you been baptized?"

Nervously, she shook her head *no*. He continued, "Will you accept Jesus as your Lord right now before your friends?" Mary balked. Jennings continued until Mary openly cried and quickly left the room. As the group began singing a song, I slipped out of the room and headed home. There was something about that experience I found troublesome. The first chance I could find, I would ask Rev. Shepherd many questions which were spinning around in my mind.

Rev. Shepherd suggested a kinder approach to help guide individuals seeking faith. "Be patient. Be soft-spoken. Offer a few pertinent Scriptures. Help the person gradually come to believe. Never try to push, pull, cajole. Your love, God's Word, and His Spirit will do the work. Trust Him. Trust Him."

Our evening sessions continued until one evening, Rev. Shepherd looked at me and said, "Luke, you have the kind of faith it takes to be a minister." Those words registered. They lingered. *Faith to be a minister. A minister...minister?* He also gave me passages of Scriptures to read and suggested I pray a lot.

On numerous evenings, Rev. Shepherd's words led me to the flood wall. Looking into the starlit sky, I questioned those *faith to be a minister* words over and over. I think I actually verbalized out loud, so I looked around hoping no one was around to hear me. "God, are you out there? Where are you? Can you hear my calling? Are you talking to me?" Reflecting, I thought how Rev. Shepherd said nothing about being intelligent or good-looking. By that criteria, I could qualify for a forest ranger or guide. *Only a powerful, caring God could have made those millions of stars,* I thought. I simply wanted to be a minister like Rev. Shepherd. I rationalized, *God called Jeremiah who said he was only a boy, Moses who had trouble talking, and disciples who were fishermen.*

Once home, I picked up my Bible and read one of the passages Rev. Woods suggested: Genesis 8, "When I look at the heavens, which you have made…what is man that you are mindful of him…"

More weeks were spent on the Flood Wall before I asked Rev. Shepherd, "What must I do to become a minister like you?"

He answered slowly, "There is a lot for you to prepare. But you only take one step at a time. I will help you. One big thing is for you to attend college. That could be your first step."

"College? I have never liked school. You know that. But I am willing to try."

"You can do all things through Christ who strengthens you," he quoted.

Weeks of wrestling followed until that momentous day finally arrived, "Nani, I am going to quit my job at Sylvania and attend college. I plan to become a minister."

"Luke, are you crazy? You have a good job. Who put that dumb idea in your head? You are making a terrible mistake! It takes money to go to college. You will not get a penny from your dad."

"Nani, I have made up my mind."

Nani turned around and started to leave, turned back, and sharply said, "Luke, pack up your clothes and leave this house."

Courage came upon me from somewhere. "Nani, I will not! You pack my clothes and place the suitcase at the door. You told your sisters and neighbors that Jack and Nancy packed up and left. I will tell your sisters you packed my clothes and kicked me out! Otherwise, I stay right here!"

Nani stormed out of the room. I stayed. Besides, where would I go? The world out there is a foreign place.

Home atmosphere was cool, sometimes icy. I hoped Dad would come to my rescue. He did not. When Christmas rolled around, a ray of sunshine shined through; Nani gave me a pair of underwear with a slight smile.

Walking into the college world was like entering a forest where I had never hunted before—frightening—but at the same time, exciting. The dean of admissions looked over my high school records, paused, and said, "You are admitted, but you will have to take a non-credited bonehead English course the first year." Religion was my major, and Philosophy was minor. A retired English teacher from the church helped some, but more spelling and not proper grammar was learned from *red marks* on written tests. First *A* came in speech class. The final was a poem I quoted without notes or lectern. Knees shook against each other as I looked at the class and quoted verbatim: "Abou Ben Adhem may his tribe increase..." by Leigh Hunt.

Friends from the Sub District Fellowship encouraged me to join the Marshall Student Christian Association. Slowly, this neophyte began to feel at home. By my junior year, the honor roll status was achieved. In the meantime, Dad helped me find employment at Owens Glass Company where he worked as a mold maker craftsman. This small 131-pound beginner worked in a hot loft throwing scrap cardboard into a casket-sized bin until it held 800 lbs. It was tied with bailing wire, rolled by hand onto a cart, and pushed to a railroad car. Promotion to a box cutter and conveyor belt unmercifully cut both hands.

Dad influenced the foreman to move me to a box-folding machine. Harry, the leader, knew the machine inside and out. He also knew every part of the human body which he enjoyed explaining. Every morning, he detailed his nightly experiences with his girlfriend in the back of his old Ford. The pictures he painted conjured up images of a garbage dumpster. The plant had a reputation of adulterous relationships, vulgarity, and gambling. Those summers added to my understanding of another part of the real world.

When time came to elect a new president for the Student Christian Association, two names were presented: James and Luke. Sue asked both of us to leave the room to allow the group to consider the candidates. The first vote was a tie. On a third vote, Luke was elected. Immediately, council meetings were set for 6:30 a.m. each Tuesday. It was a wonderful opportunity to think creatively. There would be weekend retreats, guest speakers, and cookouts. Previous years in the church taught me that church did not need to be dull. For freshman week, it was food booths, a band, dancing, and abundant fliers of forthcoming activities. The first program was presented by the campus pastor for which we later gladly gave him full credit. It was in two parts. One evening, the subject was "Reasons to experience sex before marriage." The auditorium was packed. The second session was, "Reasons to Refrain from Sex Before Marriage." About thirty attended. The pastor's absence at subsequent executive meetings was welcomed.

One senior girl caught my attention. She was very kind and a devout Christian. We talked late into the evenings. At the age of twenty-three, I still had an eleven o'clock curfew. From her house, it was a thirty-minute fast drive home. I was usually running late. Dad made it a habit of crawling out of bed to check the kitchen clock. Circumstances required some creativity.

The answer: simply turn back clock hands one hour, stay awake, wait for Dad to get up, and go back to bed and then return to reset the clock. It worked, except for the time I fell asleep. The next morning, the discrepancy was discovered. They concluded that electricity had gone off. Years later, the secret was shared.

Joyce called one afternoon asking for a favor, "Luke, Nel, my cousin from Alabama, is visiting. I need a date for her. You will like her. Come to my house at 6:00 p.m., and the four of us will go to a movie. Please help me."

"Okay, Joyce. I will do this for you."

We sat in the living room a few minutes to get acquainted. When Joyce's father entered, he gave me a lukewarm greeting. With arms crossed, he stared me in the eye and said, "Have a good time." Then came the shocker: "If you get into her pants, you will marry her. Understand?"

With red face, I responded, "Yes, sir. Yes Sir."

Joyce quickly responded, "Dad! We are simply going to a movie and coming home. Besides, we are late. We need to get going."

Sitting in the movie, one thought prevailed: *college first, seminary second.* When it is the right time, God will point the right girl out for me. Duke University was my choice among seminaries. There was nothing profound about the decision. A friend recommended it. My sister Nancy and family were closer. With a master's degree from Marshall College, I applied and was accepted along with a summer church work scholarship.

Nani asked, "How do you think you will get there, Son? You have no car, and I am sure your dad will not take you."

"Nani, I will hitchhike. Or I am sure Greyhound buses travel that far. I have saved a little money. I will just do it. Period."

The Greyhound clerk explained, "It is about 400 mi. and will take about eight hours.

The trip was an experience. I had never been that far by myself. I had never seen the place, and I knew no one there. "Luke," I said to myself, "step out in faith. That is what the disciples of Jesus did. Christian ministry is my goal. God will be with me."

It seemed the big bus stopped at every crossroad service station. Restrooms were marked "Whites Only." Another one was designated for blacks. I started toward the rear of the bus. The driver stopped me and pointed to my seat near the front. When black people entered, they automatically moved to the back. A part of me cringed.

Seminary was financially, academically, and emotionally challenging. In all categories, this young novice was ill-prepared. There was only one choice: try harder, stay up later, and pray. Occasionally, a letter arrived from home with a $10 bill enclosed. One evening, Aunt Myrtle called, "Luke, your dad is seriously ill. The doctors say he will die soon. You need to come home soon."

"Yes, Myrtle, I will fly home tomorrow. Hope to see you. Love you." A Dukie friend invited me for dinner the next day and made plans for the flight. His wife prepared a delicious chicken dinner with all the trimmings. The plane was a small single engine. We hit turbulent winds. The paper sack came in handy—so much for that good dinner.

Nani was in tears. As orderlies rolled Dad down the hall, he feebly raised his hand as if to say goodbye. "Dad, I will be praying for you," I whispered. Hours seemed like an eternity. I called Jack and Nancy whom Dad had not seen or heard from for years. "God," I prayed, "heal Dad. Give him another chance." Each day following surgery to remove fluid from his lungs, Dad was better. In three weeks, he went home.

During another visit, I turned to Dad and said, "Your life has been spared. You are alive now. Will you thank God and accept Christ as your Lord and Savior? Will you start going to church?"

An awkward pause followed. "Luke, if God wants me to be a Christian, he will make me one. It is up to God."

"But you can decide," I answered. He waved be away. One thing Dad learned from the Presbyterian minister: predestination. It was then I knew: this young seminarian still has a lot to learn.

A year and half of school still faced me. Where is that girl I had come to believe God would show me? Had God forgotten?

Would the master designer come through? Should He? I could still be a minister like Rev. Woods. I am twenty-six. Not one girl came close to the picture God etched on my mind. There were few women in seminary. Undergraduate students lived on another campus. I pondered, *Be patient.* The Bible says God keeps promises. God does.

I found her at a Halloween dance. Or did God find her? There she was. I knew immediately. There she was on the dance floor in front of my eyes. I asked, "May I?" We danced. Rather, my clumsy feet moved.

"What is your name?" I asked. Her name was quickly forgotten. Her phone number, I said over and over in my mind until it was permanently etched.

The next evening, I dialed the special number. Freddy answered. I asked, "May I speak with—your sister?"

"I have no sister," he replied.

"Well, I met this young lady at the dance last night—and I can't recall her name." Freddy sensed I needed help.

"You must want Darlene because the other one has a boyfriend and is engaged. I will get Darlene." It took some convincing, but after a few words of introduction, she agreed to date. The first date was to Morehead Planetarium in Chapel Hill to see the Star of Bethlehem show. We held hands. She squeezed. The favor was returned. There were stars other than those on the planetarium dome.

We met nearly every evening after she left her position as head nurse on the third floor of the hospital. After a fast-food stop, we found our favorite parking spot on campus. With a surge of nerve, I said, "Darlene, I love you very much and want you to be my wife." Handing the diamond to her, nervous words followed, "Will you marry me?" There was no hesitation. Hugs, kisses, and tears followed.

The next challenge followed a few days later. Her brother-in-law arrogantly announced, "It is a law around here. You have to ask Mr. Aiken permission to marry his daughter."

Marching promptly to his small grocery store, I stated my purpose, "Do you mind if I marry Darlene?"

He nodded approval followed with "What do you think about those *Niggers* playing baseball with the Durham Bulls?"

For a moment, my mind froze. After an awkward pause, Dr. Dick's recent lecture on pastoral counseling came to mind: "Resist answering patients directly. Rather, pause, give a *hum* sound and ask 'What do you think?'" Mr. Aiken took thirty minutes to express his heated thoughts. Seminary training had paid dividends.

The 7:00 p.m. wedding was in her small, frame, one room Baptist church. At 6:20 p.m., the heavens released a deluge of water. Groom, best man, and minister were parked behind the church waiting for the moment. There was no canopy, only automobile, torrential rain, and the church door.

On cue, Mickey said, "It is time. Get out now. I will open the church door." Inside, we stepped directly onto the chancel looking like drenched campers in penguin-like tuxedos. The wedding was beautiful. On her wedding band was engraved, "Each for the other." My band read, "Both for God." God had kept His promise. Together, we would serve our Maker.

We moved into a nice three-room apartment close to the hospital. Her salary helped with seminar tuition. Only one dispute surfaced: I had spotted a small creek. Bullfrogs bellowed as if calling me on a water-wading hunt. After dark, Mickey, my best man, and I pushed through overhanging brush into a small stream.

Mickey nervously asked, "Are there snakes in here?"

"Come on, Mick. We will be fine. We have our gigs to bush the brush away and scare any creatures. Don't worry. You carry the burlap sack. I will catch frogs." With flashlight beam aimed at the creatures' eyes, fifteen jumbo bullfrogs were dropped into a burlap sack. Near midnight, we slipped in the back door. One fat fifteen-inch pop-eyed frog was placed on the kitchen counter where it obediently sat as if frozen.

Mickey inquired, "What in the world are you doing?"

"I can't let Darlene miss out on our manly catch."

"But she is asleep," Mick warned.

"Don't fret, buddy." As sleepy-eyed wife stepped through the kitchen door, that old frog awakened and took a long leap toward her feet. She screamed. The leaping creature scurried to the bedroom. Dick quickly said, "See you tomorrow. Goodbye."

With master of divinity degree, we traveled to the West Virginia Annual Conference at Wesleyan College for the first time. "Darlene," I ask once more, "are you still willing to move to West Virginia?"

"Yes, we will go together. It will be interesting. I will miss my family and friends, but I am with you."

"Darling, District Superintendent Dr. Roe made arrangements to meet us Monday in the chapel before worship hour."

Dr. Roe was easy enough to identify. He was tall, broad shouldered, and dignified. "Luke, the bishop and cabinet have assigned you to the New Martinsville Charge. It is a growing community with plenty of industry and new housing developments. The present church is very small and old. The other church 4 mi. away is smaller. We would like for them to merge and build a new sanctuary.

"The General Board of Missions has granted $10,000 for seed money to inspire the congregation to get started. We feel you would be a good fit for that situation. Also, they have a lovely new parsonage which will be next to the new church. You can move in next week. I will keep in touch. Feel free to call me."

"I will. Thanks for the opportunity."

As we parted, I reflected, "Many distractions over the last several years has not dimmed my calling. Find individuals, much like Rev. Woods found me: 'Encourage them to accept Christ as Lord, surround one's self with believers, and grow. Be patient. Believers will find an exciting new life.'"

The church was indeed a small frame, poorly maintained building. It had thirty active members. A retired farmer, Henry Hicks, started the pot-bellied woodstove each Sunday morning. They welcomed us warmly.

The first person to visit us in the parsonage was Jill with her nursing infant. After introducing herself, she explained the black ink around her nipple, "The ink is to discourage my baby from nursing."

After breakfast the next morning, I said, "Darling, we are going to help the people build a beautiful sanctuary. Jesus said go door-to-door. That is what we can do. Or I am comfortable going one by one. God will be with me. Tonight, the trustees will meet to talk about securing a bank loan and finding a contractor.

"I am interested in doing something about the deep depression behind our land. I would love to get it filled to create more parking space. While visiting, I can talk to Mr. Hicks. He is a farmer and may have a tractor to cut high ground and shove it into the valley. 'All things are possible.' Let's pray about it."

The trustee meeting was long. Darlene stayed up later than usual to inquire. "Please tell me, how did it go? You look weary."

"In several ways, it was a good meeting. The progressive plans were approved. That is wonderful. However, one member adamantly balked. Mr. Thornburg was the only one to speak against borrowing $200,000, and he did not care for the contractor they suggested."

"Luke, try to understand Les. Remember how your Nani could tell where you had been by mud on your shoes? Les's actions explain a great deal about his past. Likely, his younger hardworking years were difficult. Older people are often conservative. Be patient."

"Darlene, I should be able to understand his position. We are conservative too, but when it comes to God's house and reaching out to draw outsiders, we need church appeal. Rev. Woods once warned me that every church has *an-againster*. All in all, it was a good night and perhaps time for some good rest. Love you."

The next afternoon, Henry was sitting under an oak tree sipping water. I decided to join him. "Luke, I am not making much progress," he reported. "My old tractor keeps breaking down. Not sure how much longer we can keep it going. We may have added eight or ten feet to the width of our lot, but it seems like a futile task."

"Henry, what you say we take a break for a few days? We will think it over next week. You have done a wonderful piece of work."

Henry continued telling me about the state prison a few miles away. He paused, "By the way, do you know that man walking this way?"

When he drew near, a sturdy fellow in coveralls and a hard hat introduced himself, "I am superintendent of the highway project about five miles south of here where the mountainside slid on the road. I would like to ask you a favor. The state superintendent is unhappy with my work.

"It would be helpful if you could write him a note explaining the importance of our work is to your community. A nice note could possibly save my job." With more information about his work, I promised to write the note.

As he started to walk away, I called, "Mr. Jackson, wait a minute. Tell me more about that rock slide. Would your workers have extra dirt and rocks you could bring up here and pour into that valley back there?"

"Well, yes, preacher. We need to find a place to get rid of a lot of rocks and dirt. That is my job. I can start soon to send our large dump trucks this way. We can help each other that way." Later, I was happy to tell Darlene the meaning of all those large dump trucks. "Darling, I am unsure of the theology, but Jesus did say, 'If you have faith the size of a grain of mustard seed, you can move mountains.' What do you think, Dear?"

In eighteen months, the Bartow Construction Co. had finished their work. The church, with its tall white steeple, was impressive. Twenty more feet had been added to the parking lot. The trustees had their monthly meeting to review various business matters. John Long brought plans for new padded pews. Quickly, Les Thornburg stood up and strongly opposed,

"We are too much in debt now. We must wait a few more years for such an adventure John proposes."

After a brief discussion, I chimed in, "Mr. Chairman, our beautiful church deserves new pews. The old ones have cut marks and carved initials on them. Underneath, they are caked with chewing gum. The old ones can be used in the basement fellowship hall for Sunday school classes and dinners."

Les intruded, "Norman, I mean, Mr. Harris, I move we forget the new pew idea for now." A second followed and passed. After the meeting, I spoke to the chairman. "Mr. Harris, I want to find individuals who will sponsor enough pews for our church."

Mr. Harris quietly responded, "Go for it." John offered his help. Within six months, the new padded pews were installed.

Henry who had worked so long and hard on the parking lot stood at the church door every Sunday, rain or shine. With his large weathered hands, he greeted visitors with a big smile. John helped direct traffic. Les Thornburg ushered guests and was quick to point out the comfortable padded pews. Exhausted that evening, I suggested, "Darling, it has been a God-blessed day. Suppose we retire early tonight."

Deep into the night, there was a punch into my ribs. Half awake, I said, "Darling, why are you hitting me? Can't you sleep?"

"Luke," she whispered, "I believe someone is in our house. I heard strange noises like someone messing in the kitchen downstairs."

"Sweetheart, it is likely the highway traffic. Those big coal trucks sometimes vibrate the house. I should not have told you Henry's stories about the prison."

"Luke, stop it. This is serious. There, did you hear that?"

"Yes, yes, Sweet. I did hear something like kitchen pots clanging."

"Why don't you call the police now? Do something. Oh, no, the phone is in the kitchen where the noise seems to be."

"Okay, I will get my gun from under the bed and check it out."

As I slowly inched down the steps, the sound occurred again. I turned the shotgun safety off. A shiver ran up my spine. Would I actually shoot someone? When I peeped around the corner into the kitchen, no one was there. Was someone outside the back door? I will turn on the outside lights and open the door. The light will likely frighten if anyone is there. With door open, I could see nothing except the large shaking garbage can by the maple tree. The can shook and clanged. With gun pointed, I marched forward until I realized it was a large gray-and-white snarling opossum. That innocent creature had simply sought a midnight snack. He was set free from his maximum prison and fled. I returned to a cozy bed to explain my heroic efforts.

"Darling, the sun is up, and, for obvious reason, we slept late. I have a lot on my mind. This is Ash Wednesday. After breakfast, would you see if we have a tall white candle?"

Still half asleep, she mumbled, "Luke, what in the world are you planning? Is it another one of your crazy creative ideas?"

"Dear, wait a minute, you are creative with your cooking and especially deserts. I think it important to crouch good food of the Bible in a way to make it interesting. Also, I need one of your cake pans and a little tinfoil."

"Luke, please tell be your plan."

"Okay, I plan to have individuals write a personal sin or two on a small piece of paper. They will come to the altar, light it in the Christ candle flame, and place it in the cake pan. I will speak about God's grace. You will love it."

Before the service, I had the props in place. The cake pan with tinfoil was placed on the new chest-high blond baptismal font. At the proper time, lights were dinned, and the ceremony began. The plan seemed perfect. The sins were incinerated by holy fire. Worshippers were first inspired then fearful as flames leapt higher and higher. Paper and hot wax was on fire. Sensing potential danger, our young dentist sprang from his seat and covered the flaming pan of burning sins with his clipboard. The flaming inferno was extinguished. Only holy smoke remained. Service continued.

Early the next morning, I returned to retrieve the props only to discover a deep black charred indentation on top of the baptism font. "Oh." I thought. "What will Les Thornburg say now?" I will wait until after breakfast and report to Darlene.

"Darling, thanks for a good breakfast, but guess what? The fire carved a deep black scar in the baptism font. My job today is to sand and sand and sand. There will be no visitation today."

"Well, Luke, what do you think of your great creative worship idea now?"

"Lovely, please be kind."

That afternoon, Dr. Roe called, "Luke, let me thank you for doing a great job. I need someone to plan our summer youth camps. With your past experience as a youth leader, you would be perfect, will you?"

"Dr. Roe, thank you for those nice words. But, sir, I have intended to ask you for another appointment. Darlene and I have been here four years. The church is doing well. With our low salary, it is tough to make ends meet. Besides, I would like a new challenge. Would you kindly consider what you and the cabinet can do for us?"

"Luke, I will bring your situation before the cabinet next week when we meet."

Two weeks later, Dr. Roe reported back.

"Darlene, the DS called and says he has a new appointment for us. It is in Parkersburg, an urban setting. The church location will give us opportunities to reach more people for Christ. Actually, we will need to find some boxes and begin packing in a couple weeks."

"Hold on, Luke. I have been told that churches are now supposed to pay for packing and moving. Did you know that?"

"Yes, Dear, I don't want to walk in and hand the treasurer a moving bill. I want to get off to a good start with our new congregation. We will rent a *U*-haul. I am sure brother Jack will come from Columbus and help us. We can do it."

"Luke, what about his dog?"

"Darling, Candy is well-trained. She will be no trouble."

Moving Day Is Taxing and Exciting

The *U*-haul was parked in the alley behind the parsonage. We began unpacking when Darlene called from the back door, "Luke, we have a visitor. Come." As I approached, she whispered, "Her name is Miss Goodwin, a long-standing member of the official board."

As I entered the back door, Cindy darted past me. When Miss Goodwin stood to shake my hand, Cindy jumped onto the sofa directly behind her and made a large puddle. At that instant, Miss Goodwin bent backward to sit in the urine-soaked sofa. In a flash, I reached and grabbed the church matriarch around the waist to keep her from falling or sitting.

"Oh, Miss Goodwin, I am so sorry (at the same time wondering what was going through her mind). Miss Goodwin, the dog belongs to my brother from Ohio. He is helping us move. He will be going home tomorrow. Here, why don't you sit in this high-back chair?"

"Luke, I thank you. I am fine. The people around here call me Miss Nan. That is what I would like you to call me too. Luke, I have brought you a welcoming gift. Unwrap it carefully. My grandmother gave it to me when I was a small girl. Obviously, that was a long time ago. Look at the picture and read the text."

Holding it gently, I said, "Miss Goodwin, I mean, Nan, it is lovely and meaningful. The lion and the calf with a small child leading them. I have always liked the text Isaiah 11:6. This is a tremendously generous gift. I will treasure it. Thank you."

Before she left, Miss Nan gave me a list of the church officers and explained, "The finances are stable. We pay our conference apportionments every month. The church could use some maintenance. Attendance is just okay, but the sanctuary is large enough to hold another hundred or more."

"Miss Nan, my plan is to become acquainted with the church members and visit door-to-door. With God's help, we will increase the attendance. Please come back often."

The very next day, I introduced myself to the mail carrier. "Do you live nearby?" I asked.

"Yes, my wife and I live just up the street about a block away," he warmly responded.

"Have children?" I continued.

"Yes, two teenage daughters."

"Does your family attend church? If not, I would like for you to visit our church. I am the new pastor. I would love to have you visit. I plan to start a youth group soon. We will have a good time. They would enjoy it. Please consider visiting."

When I took the mail in the house, I impulsively asked Darlene, "Will you help me start a youth group? I want to start one soon. You will help me, won't you?"

"Yes, Dear. You, of course, know I don't have other things to do like scrub the cabinets, vacuum, wash clothes and…"

"Thank you. I knew you would. I will get news in the city newspaper, our church bulletin, and make an appeal Sunday. I will get names of our church young people and phone numbers. Would you call some of them?"

"We will have a group together before you know it." I know what I will preach Sunday. My text will be Mathew 19:14: Let the little children come unto me."

"Fine, Luke, go for it."

"Now I am going to the office and outline thoughts for our trustees meeting tonight at seven."

After a brief prayer, I asked, "Trustees, I would like to ask you a favor tonight. A number of people have mentioned a need for maintenance repairs and physical appeal improvements. Would each of you write down some of the things you feel need accomplished?

"Think of things that might be accomplished in five years or more. Sheets of paper and pens are on the table. Take about ten minutes. We will have a discussion. Take the ideas home and ask your family. Bring your ideas back for the next meet."

Some of the ideas were modest and some extensive. They were presented to the official board by Ed, chair of the trustees. He had them written on newsprint: Build a ramp for those with physical handicaps, refurbish, beautify the sanctuary, lower the chancel, change the chancel backdrop, place a larger cross there, and enhance the narthex. Ed reminded them that they are long-range plans, even five years or more away.

Jim stood and asked to comment, "I am excited about your plans. Why wait five years? We need to move forward. I am willing to help see it through beginning very soon. My business has been going well. I offer $40,000 to get things going."

People applauded. Ed continued, "Jim, we thank you. You have made a generous offer. We will turn their ideas back over to the trustees for further review. Treasurers report please."

"Mr. Chairman, all bills are paid. Conference apportionments are paid in full each month."

Ed continued, "I understand our new youth president has a report. When Chad finishes, let us join for a desert afterward."

"We are happy to report that twelve youth meet each Sunday evening. Chad's father, Bill, is going to get a truck load of apples in the mountains next week. We are going to package and sell them. You can place your order tonight if you want. We plan to use our money for an Appalachian Service project in the mountains of Kentucky next year."

During refreshments, I asked Jim if I could come by his home tomorrow. "Luke, please do. I will be home after seven tomorrow evening. Hope to see you."

The evening conversation was delightful. His wife was hospitable. We talked about our families. Jim volunteered his story, "Luke, I was nearly broke. I went to our revival one night. I put my last cent in the offering plate. When the visiting evangelist gave an altar call, I went forward, knelt, and gave my life to Christ.

"I tell you, from that day, I felt like a new man. One job opportunity after another opened up. I soon had enough to purchase another truck. With a bank loan, Betty and I bought a hilltop outside of town. With a rented bulldozer, we began to slice it down. Of all things, we hit a twelve-inch seam of anthracite coal."

"Jim," I inserted, "that is a high grade of coal, I think."

"Luke, it is the highest grade. We creamed enough out of that hill to pay off the loan and build the strip mall. Things have never been better. One little difficulty: One day while excavating, a couple sticks of dynamite blew a few tons of rocks over the main highway. We settled with the state. My office is in the mall. Drop by sometime."

"Jim, thank you again. Let's have a prayer of gratitude. I will visit your office in the near future."

Darlene was half asleep when I returned. As she rolled over, she asked about my visit with Jim. "Dear, let me tell you in the morning."

After breakfast, I explained in detail Jim's conversion and road to success.

"Luke," she responded, "we are not surprised. God's Word is full of miracles. God works wonders, period."

"Dear, I agree, but the critical side of my mind kicks in. Consider this. It was Jim's faith that led him to the altar. He had an important part."

"Luke, who gave Jim faith in the first place? You understand the Holy Spirit was working in him before kneeling at the altar."

"Dear, you are sooo helpful. You have given me an idea. Sunday I may preach on the size of a mustard seed, Mathew 17:20. I will work on it in the office this morning. In the afternoon, I plan to visit."

"Luke, your mind never stops. You are allowed to slow down once in a while. I love you."

"My dear, I tell you what, I am going to take Friday off. We are going out for a nice evening dinner."

A number of our shut-ins lived in the hillside community. Two children were playing in the narrow street. I stopped and introduced myself. "What are your names?" I asked.

"I am Mark, and this is my sister Jane." Pointing, they added, "We live in that house."

"Are your parents' home?"

"No, but I will tell them that you stopped. They will be home in a little while. They are down over the hill at the Pit Place," Mark added.

"Thank you." For some reason, I was moved to find the Pit Place. Upon entering a smoke-filled room, the thought occurred, *How will I recognize their parents?* Then came a brilliant thought: they will likely resemble their children (amazing). I looked up and down the bar and then the booths. There they were.

"Are you the parents of Mark and Jane?"

"Yes, why?"

"I'm Reverend Luke. I had a nice visit with your lovely children on the street this afternoon. I wanted to meet you, get acquainted, and invite you to church sometime. We have good children's classes."

"Reverend, let us order you something to drink. What would you like?"

"Thank you. A cold Coke would help. It has been a long hot day."

"Reverend, we are not going to church now. The children used to sing in a children's choir. Mary, in particular, has a very good voice, if I may say so. We will think about your visit and invitation."

"If you don't mind, I will tell Martha, our music director, about your children. I will get you on our mailing list, so you can see the many opportunities. I hope to see you soon. I will pray for your family."

After breakfast the next morning, I surfaced a subject which had been on my mind for a long time. "Darlene, everything is going along so well it occasionally makes me nervous."

"Why? Tell me."

"You remember those words about *an-againster* in every church? I keep wondering where that person might be. I haven't seen one yet."

"Luke! Where is your faith? Let's not let doubt get in the way of God's good work. Besides, if one of those so-called *againsters* shows up, you and God can handle it. We will be okay. Keep the faith, Luke, okay?"

At the next board meeting, a healthy progress report was presented. Progress on the sanctuary was moving along. Martha announced the beginning of a children's choir. Chad explained next summer's youth Appalachian service trip, "With the apples we sold plus a nice gift, we have half of the money to rent a bus. Some of you may want to contribute. We hope to have about thirty kids. A few are from other churches. We are so excited."

After the meeting, I asked Bill to walk to the parking lot with me.

"Bill, we are reaching new people for Christ every week. But Bill, there are still a lot of people out there unrelated to Christ and Christian fellowship. How could we reach beyond our church walls? I would like for you to brainstorm with me."

"Luke, to begin with, we could canvass the community, hand out pamphlets, knock on doors. Jesus said, 'Go into all the world,' didn't he?"

"Bill, I ran across a wild idea in our monthly evangelism magazine. A few churches have started worship services in outdoor theaters. That would be too far out for our church."

"Wait, Luke, wait. You said to brainstorm. We have an outdoor theater near here. It is about a mile from Jim's strip mall. Oh, maybe there is a setback. It is owned by a prominent Catholic businessman. We better put that idea on hold."

The next afternoon, I made it a point to visit Jim's office on the hill. Jim was not too crazy about the theater idea but added, "The owner is Nick Garbineo. He is a nice guy. He owns the restaurant near the theater."

I found Mr. Garbineo's office. "Mr. Garbineo, I am Rev. Luke. Is there a possibility our church could rent your theater to hold Sunday morning worship services? Would you be open to the idea, sir?"

After asking questions about me and our church, he continued, "Reverend, first of all, feel free to call me Nick. As for the worship service, I would need to consult our bishop in Wheeling. Besides, if people park in their cars, how could they kneel to pray? That could be a problem, but I will consult my bishop and let you know the answer in a week or two."

"Thank you, Nick."

The next two weeks did not come quick enough. "Mr. Garbineo, did you get a chance to ask your bishop?"

"Yes, I did. He had no objection. I did ask about that kneeling question. He said, 'Nick, it is not a matter of physical position. It is where the heart is.' The answer is yes. The theater is available. Let me know if there is more I can do."

"Yes, sir. I will be talking to you again soon."

First chance the next morning, I turned Darlene around to look at her in the face. With a warm hug, I said, "Sweetheart, this is our day all day. I said I would not work on Friday. So what would you like to do? Or what would you like for me to do for you? Did I actually say that?"

"Well, let's clean up the house and take a little nap before we go out to eat this evening. How does that sound?"

"Fine with me. Whatever you say. Where do we start?"

I chose a nice restaurant with candlelights and soft music in the background. After being seated, she said, "Luke, this reminds me of our early days of dating."

"What type of food would you like, Dear?"

"I want something light, like a shrimp salad."

"That is not much. You worked hard today. Then let's end up with a heavy desert."

"Luke, I have something to tell you. Yesterday the doctor informed me that...that...I am pregnant. We are going to have a baby. Luke, are you crying? Are you laughing?"

"Yes...Dear...it is a joyful cry—with a mixture of laughter. Here, have a hug and a kiss right before all of these people and God."

The next day, Bill and two members met together at the theater to evaluate our new opportunity. "Bill, obviously, there is a lot to do. I am confident our committee will help. We will need a ladder to climb to the rooftop. At least it is flat. Someone will need to arrange a microphone to connect with the car speakers. Rich, you have electrical skills. Can we count on you for that?

"There is a pump organ available. Martha will play or get her friend and try to arrange soloists. We will need four ushers for parking and the offering. I will contact funeral homes for flowers. They often throw them away. Bill, I will contact a couple of the theatre laborers to clean up early Sunday mornings. If they happen to not show up, well..."

"Luke, do you have any idea what cleaning up at a drive-in theater is like? You might not like what you find."

"Bill, how would you know?"

The next days and weeks were filled with the usual: bulletins, sermon preparation, visits, weddings, funerals, helping Darlene shop, and attending youth gatherings with her.

On July 7, the Greyhound bus pulled out of the parking lot with twenty-eight energetic teenagers and four adults. Destination was Centre College, Kentucky.

Tex Evans greeted our crew. His low-key and humorous antidotes made everyone feel welcomed. After a few more funny stories, he explained our schedule, "As you already know, you will reside here at Centre College. You will be glad to know their swimming pool will be available in the evening. Breakfast will be 7:00 a.m. Each group of ten or twelve individuals will board a van for your designated project. In the meantime, enjoy the pool and get a good night's sleep."

The next morning, the vans were out front and ready to roll. Thirty minutes later, we were out of the small town and on a narrow country road which soon became gravel and then dirt. Chad turned to me and questioned, "Where in the world are we?"

"Chad, I don't know. Yes, I do. We are in the country."

"Oh, thank you," he replied.

When we did approach a house, someone called, "Look out the window. There, there is a small girl down over the hill. I think she is picking blackberries. She is naked. Nelson, can we stop and help her?"

Nelson answered: "Not now, maybe we can stop here on our way back later."

When we arrived to the house of our assignment, he announced, "No one is supposed to be home today. The house is in bad need of repair. Of course, be careful. First, we will look the place over. Be sure to use rubber gloves. Take plastic bags for the trash."

In a few minutes, Pete returned, "Preacher, these people have been peeing from the back door. Not only is there trash, but it stinks."

After everyone was busy, I took a stroll toward a couple broken down cars. To my surprise, someone was in a front seat.

"Hi, fellow. What you doing?"

"Well, dude, this seat has a hole in it. Now do you know what I am doing?"

"Sorry, pal, I need to get back to my work team. We could use a couple more hands if you would like to help."

On our return trip, Nelson did stop at the house where the little girl had been picking blackberries. A brother and sister came out to meet us. We learned their baby sister had been picking her breakfast.

Janet noticed the hands of the brother. They were literally caked with black crud. "May I wash your hands?" Janet asked. "We have some soap in the van."

"Sure," he gladly replied. Janet held his hands. Tracy scrapped and scrubbed. She inquired, "Where are your parents?"

"Oh, they go to town every day for work. They will return this evening."

That evening after showers, dinner, and swim, individuals openly shared their personal experiences.

The week passed quickly. On the last morning for work, Tex announced, "As requested, you will have materials to build that outhouse. They will be at the site when you arrive."

"Yah, yah," the team cheered together.

It took a day to build. When finished, Chad told David a wrench had been dropped down the hole. "David, I believe you are small enough to squeeze down and get it. Would you?" David gladly accepted the challenge. When his head emerged through the hole, several *good friends* snapped his picture.

They said, "We will tell people back home what a good time we had."

Interrupting, I added, "Team, as you know I have been busy all week with you. I have not had time to prepare a sermon. Which one of you said 'Amen'? Okay, listen to this. I am calling on each of you to share your experiences with the congregation this Sunday in place of my sermon. It will likely be the best message they have ever heard. Pete, you said that amen word again."

Carpenters had nearly finished the sanctuary when we returned. Jim was already inspecting when I entered. We were both tremendously pleased.

"Luke, there is one last thing I want added. I am going to have the balcony rails painted gold. It is one more way to brighten things up. The canopy over the pulpit which you asked for will keep eggs and tomatoes from coming down on your head. Come here, I have something to show you."

"What is that?" I asked.

"Luke, this is an old glass cross. Sometime in the past, it was illuminated with small light bulbs. An electrician discovered it while crawling through spiderwebs under the chancel. He said the cross was at least twenty feet back."

"Jim, can you make sense of that? A hidden cross?"

"Miss Nan, one of the oldest members, thought she knew. She said years ago this cross hung on the chancel backdrop. A few people claimed the bright light bulbs hurt their eyes. She was reasonably sure someone decided to hide it where no one would think of looking. Well, until now."

"Jim, we need to put this cross in our history museum with the other artifacts. And Jim, this discovery would make a sermon on 1 Corinthians 1:18, 'The Hidden Cross.' However, I better save this story someday for another church. We would not want to embarrass anyone."

"Hold up, Luke. Don't even think about any idea of leaving. There is a lot more things for us to do. I have been meaning to tell you something. You have been busy for four years. You and family deserve a vacation. Before fall, I want you and family stay in our Palm Beach condo."

"Thank you, Jim. I may take you up on the nice offer."

With such a nice offer, I hurried home.

"You are home early, Luke. Lunch will not be ready for an hour. The girls are making a mess. Let me take care of them now."

"Wait, I have something important to share with you."

"It includes all of us. Jim has offered for us to use his condominium in Florida this summer. It would be a good break for all of us. Honey, would you be for it?"

"Yes, dear, but the summer is about over. How could you work it in with all the church activities and the drive-in?"

"I will get someone to handle the worship services. The lay leader will cover hospital calls. Also, Kevin, my Presbyterian friend, will cover for me if needed. Please, let us plan on the trip."

Two weeks later, we were relaxed in Jim's plush Fort Lauderdale residence when he called: "Luke, I am going to fly down tomorrow. I want you to meet me at the airport, Gate 5, at 10:00 a.m. I am going to take you sea fishing at Key West. Can you make it?"

"Yes, sir. We will be there. And the girls?"

"Relax, Luke, the girls will have a good time."

The next evening, we were comfortable in a Key West hotel talking about Earnest Hemmingway and fishing. "Luke, we will get a nice seafood dinner. Tonight we hope for a good night's sleep. Eight thirty in the morning, our boat captain will be at the pier waiting for us."

"But, Jim, tomorrow is Sunday. Fish on Sunday?

"Luke, we are going fishing, rain, shine, or whatever!"

Mid-morning, we were far out to sea. The captain's mate baited and set several lines for trolling. The morning passed. No fish. "Jim, I told you we would catch nothing during church time!"

"Luke, be patient."

About 12:30, there was a large splash forty yards behind the boat. The pole bent. The reel squealed and line sang. Fifteen minutes later, a six-feet sailfish was guided toward the stern. The mate prepared to gaffe when a large shark seized our prize and swam away with its prey. After catching our breath, Jim said, "That is okay. We will catch plenty more fish before the day is over."

When back home, June 11, Jay Henry and I were strolling and bemoaning the Methodist appointment process. Both of us knew we were going to be moved to a different charge somewhere. Jay broke several moments of silence.

"Luke, our future is not in our hands. The bishop and superintendents control our lives. I wonder how much God is actually in the process."

"Jay, I understand your feelings. I sometimes ask myself the same questions. Then I think, in a way, we are free. We could become Baptists or independent preachers. Furthermore, our friends in the corporate world experience the same frustrations as you feel. The Methodists do offer us a degree of security. We will always have employment. Besides, God is bigger than a bishop."

"Yes, Luke, but it is the uncertainty. I have my mind on a certain church and the DS says they have someone else going there. Or that minister is not moving. Or that church pays too much or little for my level of experience. Then one of my peers gets a plum because he knows the right person."

"Jay, all you say sounds accurate and true. But for a moment, let us look at it another way. We are in the ministry because God has called us. We are committed. We are driven. We are here to preach Christ and serve regardless of where we are sent. True? Okay? 'All things work together for good for those who love the Lord.'"

"Luke, we will pray for each other. And we will pray for the bishop."

About 10:00 p.m., Dr. Hensley called, "Luke, the cabinet has put you down for St. Matthew."

"Dr. Hensley, will you tell me more about the appointment?"

"Luke, St. Matthew is between two large cities. The area is growing rapidly. There is one new housing development after another being built. It is a wonderful opportunity. Presently, they have a new educational complex. They plan to build a sanctuary. Darlene will like the parsonage. The cabinet meets tomorrow morning. I need your answer tonight or very early in the morning."

"Dr. Hensley, Darlene and I will go where you think best. That is my answer."

The educational building had been well-planned. The fellowship hall was spacious. However, every weekend, folding chairs had to be set up for the worship service. Darlene was satisfied with the parsonage. Schools were close.

After furniture was in place, cabinets cleaned, and daughters' rooms decorated, Darlene asked the usual question, "What are your hopes and plans?"

"Sweetheart, I believe you already know. I will first visit church members. Later, it will be door-to-door canvassing, invite, invite, invite. Ruby, our secretary, has already prepared a large map of different neighborhoods. I have my eye on one new development. I hope to get there before winter. How is that for a start, Sweet?"

"Luke, are you going to find time for us?"

"Oh, yes, Dear. We will still have time for a night out."

"Luke, every week!"

Sunday school hour was used to train interested visitors about Christian faith in six to eight sessions: 1.) The Risen Christ; 2.) Holy Bible; 3.) Living as a Christian; 4.) Holy Spirit; 5.) UM History. After two years, 120 new members had joined.

One evening, Terry, the youth president, offered a suggestion, "I think it would be nice to have a few games other than volleyball all the time. What about a shuffle board painted on the fellowship hall floor?"

Jake added, "I would like for us to have a pool table. I mean, a regulation size one. Let us put a little spice in out gatherings."

Darlene added, "We will not forget our deeper purpose is to study and grow in Christ. As your counselor, we will have study time. And there is something else to think about. The trustees may not like your recreational ideas. Some may think they are plainly un-Christian."

"Darlene," Tray inserted, "I am willing to meet with the trustees myself. Better yet, I believe I can count on Maryland to go with me. She is persuasive. She has a way, you know. They won't be able to say no to her."

At the next board meeting, youth plans were approved.

Darlene interrupted a quiet moment following the evening snack, "Luke, you seem deep in thought. Are you feeling low? What is on your mind? Please don't keep anything from me."

"Honey, you always read my mind. Two things have stopped me in my tracks. They have sapped my energy."

"Luke, please share with me."

"You know our neighbor next door? We engaged in conversation the other morning. I was simply encouraging her to attend church services. As I pressed on, she abruptly stopped me. 'Preacher,' she said, 'you talk too much. You don't slow down to give anyone a chance to say a word. No, I will not attend your church!' Darlene, she turned and walked away."

"That hurt, didn't it? I could have approached her just like you did and had the same result. In other words, Luke, slow down. BP. Be patient. Gain a friendship. Later, an individual will likely tell you their story. You recall how your swimming pals crossed the street to avoid your pressure? Be smart."

"Dear, that is the psychological tools taught you in nursing school."

"Luke, call it what you want. We were simply taught to listen. Patients will tell a great deal about themselves if given a chance. Be patient. Listen to the heart and mind of others."

"I know. It is hard for me to slow down. I must come across as arrogant and prideful. I have preached on pride and humility.

Maybe it takes a hard rebuke like that one to really understand. Keep praying for me."

"Luke, do you want to share the other thing bothering you?"

"Dear, I may as well get it off my chest. I am embarrassed about both of these situations. As usual, be soft. I am sensitive, as you know."

"Luke, I will. I love you. We want to help each other be better witnesses. So—the other situation?"

"Darlene, after my sermon last Sunday, a regular visitor stopped me at the door. He looked me straight in the eye and spoke sharply. He said, 'Preacher, you know what happened yesterday? Do you listen to the news? I will tell you. Dr. Martin Luther King was assassinated. He was killed. You said not a word about the national tragedy. You will not see me in this church again.'

"Darling, he stabbed my heart. What he said was so true. I have failed. You need say nothing. Now I recognize my problem. I have been so busy with feet and eyes on the ground that I have been blind to the larger world. I have not been listening to the news. I know. God help me."

"Luke, God does help us. The angry fellow may have done you a favor. I know you pretty well. You are big enough to handle criticism and learn from it. We need to pay more attention to national and world news. We are human. We make mistakes, but God is still using us for his purpose.

"In the meantime, why not turn our minds toward all the good things that happened in two short years? Consider all the new members, youth activities, the delightful weddings, care for sick, and grieving. The future still looks bright."

Two days later, Bishop Strong called and asked to drop by for a visit. I thought it strange. Explaining the forthcoming visit, I commented to Darlene, "A visit from a bishop is rare. I wonder what could be on his mind. It prompts curiosity, apprehension, and a small touch of optimism in me all at the same time."

"Luke, once again, be patient. Relax. We have faith. It can only be good."

On Thursday, Bishop Strong joined us in the living room. He asked about our health, the twins, and spoke of the good things he has heard about St. Matthew. Then he hastened on to say, "Luke, the Conference Administration Council has approved an aggressive new program called 'Church Growth.' Your name and Steve Wells are suggested to lead it. That is why I wanted to personally visit and ask you.

"We believe your enthusiasm and church growth record makes you a perfect fit. Instead of one congregation, you can assist numerous churches to be more effective. What do you think? Keep in mind that you will need to move.

"Also, you will go to Columbus, Ohio, for a two weeks' training workshop. There is an allowance for you to either rent or buy a home. On June, the program and budget will be presented to the Annual Conference for approval. Again, Luke, are you interested?"

"Bishop, I thank you and others for the compliments. Darlene and I will give it serious consideration. Leaving this wonderful congregation would be difficult. We will pray and get back to you in a few days, if that is all right?"

By Thursday afternoon, ministerial appointments were for the most part set. Our hearts were racing as we pondered thoughts of a new home, packing, and a new challenge. However, there was an uncomfortable, disquieting feeling among a number of us. Steve and a few designers of the program tried to explain the possible objections. Denver spoke. "Let me tell you flat out. You know there has been and still is a power struggle among certain leaders. They are afraid the program would give one power group more influence than the other." Dale added, "I can't go that far. Some think they could find more qualified leaders than the ones chosen. They also think the financial burden on churches would be too much." Steve concluded, "The planning committee has done its part. All we can do is wait for the vote tomorrow."

After a lengthy debate, the "Church Growth" program was narrowly defeated. The final result was difficult to share with Darlene.

"Luke, what are we going to do?" she anxiously asked.

"Dear, I was able to talk with the bishop after the session. He assured me there will be an appointment somewhere sometime. Most likely, it may be an associate for a while. He hastened to add that the church has no parsonage, but Dr. Sink, a professor at the college, is leaving for his sabbatical.

"He graciously offered the use of his home. Steve, with more seniority, will get a church first. Don't worry, he said he will take care of us."

I commented to Darlene on the way home, "I have the going-to-a-funeral kind of feeling. The pit of my stomach aches. I know you hurt too. Saying goodbye to the congregation will be painful. Packing for something somewhere and an uncomfortable living situation hurts! Oh, darling, I may just travel to the Presbyterian Head Office in Columbus and ask about becoming a Presbyterian."

"Luke, yes, I hurt for us and the children as well. Somehow, we will adjust. 'All things work out for good,' you know? We are not becoming Presbyterians. Period!"

After a couple months in the professor's house, Buckhannon D. S. called, offering the parsonage on an abandoned camp ground. Once again after we had packed, he called back with upsetting news, "Luke, Bishop Strong has changed his mind."

"What now?" I asked. "Why? Can you give me an explanation? We have been going through a lot of frustration. Why? His actions are highly questionable. Why?"

"Luke, the Bishop's son-in-law from New Jersey agreed to teach at the college. He and his daughter get the camp parsonage. Sorry. Something will still work out. Please be patient. Try to understand. Most likely, Bishop Strong has his reasons. He has tough decisions to make. He also has responsibility for the college, you know. Life is not always simple. Something will still work out yet."

Darlene was upset. She gave me her usual statement of faith: "BP. Let us give it time. We are still alive. We know to whom we belong."

A New Appointment
One year later

"Darlene, we have good news. The bishop has kept his promise. Bishop Strong called and offered us an appointment. The church is in a bedroom community of a large city. He said the church has been static for a few years. He thinks we can inject some life into it."

"Luke, I do appreciate his confidence is us. He is not God. I would like to tell him to remember that Christ is the source of life. Without His Spirit, our work is in vain. Otherwise, all else is vain."

"Dear, Dear, slow down, relax. While you catch your breath, let me add to your theology. Jesus said, 'My Father works still, and I work.' Get this, 'The Lord works still, and Darlene and Luke work.' Amen."

"Luke, I didn't ask for a sermon. Best we get there first and check the situation out with our own eyes."

Once the *U*-haul drove off, Darlene breathed a sigh and said, "Luke, we finally have a parsonage. Well, unless the *powers that be* change their minds! This will be our home. Members have brought food. Let's eat."

"Darling, I have an idea for my first sermon."

"Luke, your mind is at work already. Slow down. What is your idea, Dear?"

"The title will be 'Ground Zero: Ready for Lift Off.'"

"Dear sermon maker, where did that title come from?"

"Darlene, remember we have been watching TV rockets on the news lately."

"While we relax a few minutes, would you like expanding on the big idea?"

"My Dear positive critic, it is not developed yet. First we will take a look at our grounding. Christ is the starting point. Secondly when we deeply acknowledge to whom we belong, we will be ready to move out to witness and serve. To say 'I am a member of a church' is not an adequate foundation for life. Christians need to be grounded in Christ and the Holy Word. How about that?"

"Preacher boy, it has promise."

"After the sermon, I will call for a combined board meeting and planning session. Once leaders are involved with their own ideas, they will likely be ready to move forward. Like in our last church, it did not take long to achieve their goals."

Six months later

"Darlene, over a short time, consider where the church has come. A part-time secretary is employed. Letters were sent to potential teenagers in the community. The conference located a potential seminary student for summer employment. He was willing to come. The church pays half and the conference half.

"Wednesday study and prayer group is meeting. A few books were donated, and a library was started. The suggestion for a dance class was delayed for further discussion. A visitation program is in the planning. The minister and secretary will be in the office by 9:00 a.m. with exception for emergencies."

"Dear, I called the student. His name is Kevin. He plans to visit us Sunday for worship and hoped his long hair down to shoulders will be no problem. I assured him all will be fine. He has musical talent, plays the piano, and has directed plays in his home church. Our youth will love him.

"An additional note, Denver Miles, editor of the *Conference* paper, has asked me to submit an article on how I lead council planning sessions. Maybe tomorrow I can get it off to him. It is hard to imagine what another year will bring."

The next morning involved an experience which that evening I planned to share with Darlene. "Darlene, my office morning was interesting. Let me tell you a story that is, as usual, ours and only ours. First about three weeks ago, a young man visited very upset. He nervously said his girlfriend was pregnant, and he was afraid he would be forced to marry her.

"We had a long discussion. I tried my best to share what knowledge I had about a woman's physiology (much thanks to you). I asked him to delay a commitment for a few weeks and come back to see me. He came back today delighted to tell me she is not going to have a baby. We then spent a great deal of time talking about faith and commitment to Jesus. Both of us left happy. Dear, what would I do without you to share these experiences? Thanks."

"Luke, now I have a story you may be able to explain. The secretary told me someone spent a night on the parlor sofa. Do you know about that? It frightened Patricia. You did not tell me."

"Yes, it did happen. I walked past the parlor the other morning and had a double take. I awakened him. After questions, we went to McDonalds for a ham, egg, cheese, biscuit, and invited him to our 11:00-a.m. worship. If a young person asks me about life in ministry, I will tell him, 'It will not be dull.'"

"Luke, please don't make light of this. There could be danger!"

"Dear, we need to go beyond normal. The church must go beyond its walls to reach people for Christ. Jesus never said being a disciple was going to be easy. We love what we are doing."

"Luke, sometimes, I feel a need to get myself beyond four walls of this house and church. Angelia came home from school crying yesterday. I may need to talk to her teacher, or maybe you need to visit the school."

"Darlene, you are carrying a heavy load. I am sorry. It is my fault. We need to get away for a while. Friday night, we will go out for dinner. Better yet, our conference newsletter had a forthcoming trip of the Holy Land. The good part is that if we recruit sixteen people, we both can go free. Interested?"

"It sounds like a pipe dream to me!"

"Darling, nothing ventured, nothing gained. I will call next week for more information."

"Don't forget, Dreamer, you have two daughters. What about them?"

"Sweetheart, faith, faith, faith, hope, and that other word, love. I love you very much. In the meantime, this is our family weekend coming up. What about a picnic lunch at the city park on Saturday and perhaps a swim?"

"Luke, is cereal okay for breakfast? Angelia and Kate have already eaten."

"A light breakfast is fine. Afterward, I head off to our quarterly district conference. They will have something to eat there. I also have a meeting with Brian for a light lunch."

"What do you do at district conference?"

"Darling, I am running a bit late. Do you mind if we debrief our day at bedtime tonight?"

The day was long. At bedtime, Darlene introduced the subject, "Luke, this is catchup time. Tell me about your day."

"Darling, you go first."

"Okay, pretty much boring. We ate. We shared family and concerns. Everyone asked to raise money to support our missionary in Kenya. It was boring, except for one thing: We will have the missionary coming to visit district churches next year. Telling about Christ in other countries excites me. I once thought about being a nurse missionary overseas. We could still go."

"Dear, we had coffee, cake, and juice. The DS welcomed a couple new ministers to our district. He gave a short sermon. You have heard him before. He is an energetic speaker. He covered conference programs and asked our support including the missionary from Kenya. He named charges that had paid their apportionments.

"Our church once again was not on the list. I told him our treasurer claimed she had paid monthly, and we have an accountant in the church reviewing the situation. Lunch with Brian was nice. He is willing to support our planned trip to the Holy Land. He is reasonably confident some of his members will be interested.

"He also shared his personal life without a wife. I didn't express my thoughts as I immediately thought of Natalie who sings in our choir. We shared sermon ideas. Say, would you be willing to have Natalie and Brian over for dinner some evening?"

"Yes, Dear, I am willing. But let's first see if they are interested. Then we can check our calendars. Let us turn over and go to sleep."

"But…well, okay." As I rolled over thinking of an evening dinner with Kevin and Natalie, the phone rang. "Hello? Yes, I will be over to the hospital as soon as I can."

"Luke, what was that all about?"

"Dear, Mertie, as you know, is a chain-smoker. She is making a lot of noise for a cigarette, but because of oxygen in the room, they will not let her. The nurse thinks I can calm her down. I will try to talk with her and the staff. We will get it worked out. I won't take long."

"Luke, why don't you delegate others? We need more private time!"

"Sweetheart, I had a dream about delegating some time ago which I will share with you later. Love you."

Friday evening after Darlene's meal, Brian said, "Darlene, this was a delicious dinner. Thank you. Maybe we could come to your place every Friday night (only joking). By the way, Luke, what happened to your finger?"

Darlene responded quickly, "Brian, Luke thinks he is still a teenager. He cannot resist playing games with our youth crew. Luke, you tell him."

"Brian, it is nothing. We were playing volleyball. I went up to spike. One of our big boys on the other side went up higher. His fist came down like a hammer on the ball. That is the story of my bruised finger."

"Luke, tell the rest of it," Darlene insisted.

"All right. The kids tried to pull, push, jerk it back in place. It did not work. The emergency room doctor put it back in its proper place. Say, let's change the subject. Natalie, would you have interest in a fun game of monopoly?"

The evening was a joy. After they left, Darlene commented, "Luke, did you notice how they had trouble keeping their eyes off each other?"

"I did. I also think Brian purposefully played the game conservatively. He wanted Natalie to do well. And she did. Dear, I think they may be a good match. Matchmaking could be a good ministry. We know a lot of people which puts us in a good position to help people meet people. 'Match maker, match maker, make me a match…'"

"Luke, you can stop." Darlene said. "You are not ready for the choir. You preach. Let others sing. Maybe tomorrow morning after breakfast, we can review the choir trip Kevin and I have been planning. Now is sleep time."

"Darling, I had trouble going to sleep last night thinking of the choir trip. Where will they find resources to go by bus? And where are they going? Catch me up."

"First Kevin has outlined our trip to the Outer Banks of North Carolina. They will perform or present songs from Dangerfield in a large tent at Nags Head. Kevin will preach. That will be a unique experience for all of us. As for the money, Kevin and Foster want to have a yard sale.

"He recommended reducing the price on each item every thirty minutes. He says they usually get rid of everything before the day is over. The administration board will surely help some. Likely, churches where they present *Danger Field Newby* will take up an offering for them. Also, we can ask our youth to pay something. Faith. The money will come in."

"Darling, it sounds very workable. I love the drama script, especially when they sing, 'Look out your window and see what you can see.' Actually, I have a sermon evolving from those words. The text will be St. John 9 where Jesus heals the blind man. When Jesus opens our eyes and hearts, we see wonderful new things.

"You, Kevin, and youth spread the Word outside, and I will stay here and challenge the congregation to look for opportunities beyond our church windows. Brian and I plan to have lunch together. Hopefully, he has a few people signed up for the Holy Land trip. I know of eight people signed up from our church. Wednesday evening and weeks following, I may talk about walks Jesus took. That will take some consecrated study on my part. Maybe we can do some of the research together.

"Now concerning the missing church money. About three this afternoon Ed, the auditor, the treasurer, and I met to talk about the disappointing financial discovery. She had already admitted to her accounting errors and promised to make corrections.

"She will resign at the next board meeting explaining her age and failing eyesight. If she follows through as hoped, some of the board members will shed tears and plead for her to stay. The plan is for no one to know the circumstances except us. Pray for our meeting."

The next day, parents were at the church to see the drama team leave by bus. They were back when the bus returned a week later with their happy children.

Once home and settled in, Darlene, though exhausted, was anxious to report on their experiences in North Carolina. "Luke, all of the churches we visited gave us a warm welcome and dinner. They also took up a free-will offering for us. We were paired off in groups of two. Host parents took us to their homes for the night and gave us breakfast the next morning.

"One thing surprised us: the pastor of one church insisted the youth give a demonstration of how they walk down the aisle and then present a few minutes of the play. He explained to Kevin. He said that the church holds him responsible for the programs he brings in. Besides, members give an hour of their time. It is something he always does. Of course, we did exactly as he asked. Luke, what do you think of the minister's requirement?"

"Darlene, we are leaders. Congregations hold the minister responsible. I like the idea."

"Luke, one night, we stayed at Avon. We slept that night in the fellowship hall. That morning, the bus was loaded for a beach trip to Buxton to see the lighthouse and swim. About 3:00 p.m., we loaded the tired and water-soaked kids on the bus to return to Avon Church. Kevin counted heads. One was missing, namely Tim. A note of fear struck.

"Some went to the beach. I checked the food truck. Finally I asked a ranger to call the church for me. Rev. Jones reported that our boy was fine. When he went to the church this morning, he found Tim sleeping under a kitchen table. We were all relieved. Other than that one problem, all went exceptionally well. Obviously, you survived the week without me."

"It was tough. A couple of parents invited me to dinner. I took Brian out to dinner one night. I really did miss you and the girls. I would rather you not leave again. The first talk on Jesus's walks went well, I think."

"What walk was it?"

"It was Jesus's walk and talk with scribes in the temple. The next one will be his walk in the desert of temptation. More significantly, I learned we have enough registrations for the Israel trip. Again, our trip is free. Better yet, Natalie is willing to take care of Angelia and Kate. We will pay her. The bus will pick us up here and take us to the Pittsburg airport September 30. Think you can be ready?"

"You bet I can, Love."

"Darlene, I have a desire to take a walk along the Ohio River tomorrow. Besides needing a little exercise, there just may be an Indian point waiting for me. It would be nice to do something a little different. Would you like to come along? I will be back early. There is the wedding rehearsal at five thirty. Do you mind?"

"Not at all. You please go. I plan to take the girls shopping tomorrow. Who knows? I may find a treasure for myself. Enjoy your walk. I will enjoy mine."

My heart pressure raced with happiness as I hurried past the city park basketball court. Two teams seemed to enjoy their game. My entertainment would be at the river about a block ahead. Walking along the shore reminds me of arrow hunts with Steve along the Potomac years ago. I walked in a zigzag fashion, eyes glued to the ground, looking left and right. When something looked promising, my walking stick would turn it over for closer inspection. Time faded away into oblivion. I had moved into another world. It was like not existing at all, except when the wind picked up and the trees swayed. On those occasions, there was a feeling someone was watching. The walking stick turned over an arrowhead. With it in my hand, it said to me: "You are holding a point last touched by a warrior. He may have intended it for a deer?" For a moment, I felt like that Indian was standing beside me. The wind stirred the trees again. I turned to look. A man was standing about 30 yd. behind me. We looked at each other. "Hello there!" I said. "Are you fishing today, or are you looking for artifacts also?" He moved close.

"No," he answered. "My friends bet I could not swim across the river. I won the bet. But now I am exhausted and not sure I can swim back. Tell me, how far is the bridge?"

"Sorry, pal, the next bridge is about 4 mi. downriver. I have an idea for you. When I was a boy, we used to take a log and paddle ourselves across. I need to hurry on now. Good luck."

"Thank you. That is what I will do."

My watch said, "Hurry home. Prepare for wedding rehearsal." My mind walked faster than my feet. There was something strange about that fellow back there. I will call the police when home. But getting ready for the rehearsal must come first.

During a hurried sandwich, Darlene handed me the local morning newspaper. Front page read, "Prisoner that scrimmaged with our local athletics yesterday escaped. He was later captured on the Ohio side of the river."

"Luke, if you had not been obsessed looking for rocks, you could have given that fellow a Christian witness. Now let me tell you what treasures I found while shopping. I bought a dress for the rehearsal tonight and another one for the wedding dinner tomorrow. Angelia and Kate found dresses also. We had a great time. You may want to go looking for Indian stuff more often."

Later, flight from Pittsburg to Tel Aviv, Israel, was seventeen hours including a couple stops. In the flight, I said, "Darlene, this is the longest I have sat still in my entire life."

"Luke, I agree, but we have time to catch up on needed rest. Once we get to Israel, we will be running again. Look to your right. Bill and Nina are sound asleep."

"Dear, what do you look forward to most?"

"Luke, new sites will be fine. My chief goal is to get a bottle of Jordan water. Someday, we will baptize our grandchildren with holy water from the Jordan River. I want to shop in the Jerusalem marketplace."

"Your interests?"

"I am interested in archeological digs."

Jaffa, our Jewish tour guide, greeted us at the airport. Luggage was loaded on the bus. After courteous welcomes, Jaffa announced that our first stop would be the amphitheater at Caesarea and other sites throughout the week such as Jerusalem, Bethlehem, Calvary, the catacombs, Gethsemane, Jordon River, Masada, and Bedouin country. He paused and apologized for getting far ahead of himself.

We did move fast and saw a lot. The seven days flew by like a dream. Darlene suggested we review as we take the long air flight home.

"Darlene, let me start. We walked over land where Jesus walked. He left his footprints. We walked in the Garden of Gethsemane, to the place of the crucifixion, and to the Jordan River. You insisted I fill two wine bottles which you wanted me to carry all day. That I did."

"Luke, you will be glad someday. You read the Scripture of Jesus's baptism there. That was a highlight. The marketplace was special. I bought a twelve-piece nativity set. It took forty-five minutes to negotiate a deal. The owner chased me down the street to bring me back to offer a better price."

"Darlene, I was fascinated with engineering feats and archeological digs which give us facts about the lifetime of Jesus. Our taxi ride on that one free day showed us a bit of Bedouin life. I was saddened by the way small children had to make rugs in the factory."

"Luke, I am sleepy. I miss Angelia and Kate. I am ready for home."

"Dear, let me share some thoughts that may help you go to sleep. Much of Jesus's walk of two thousand years ago is covered by tons of stone and speculation. Now this is my most recent reflection: Jesus rose from the dead. Jesus is with us now every day, now. He is here with you and our friends. He is with Angelia and Kate now.

"Tomorrow we will walk where Jesus walks. We will think Jesus's thoughts. We will talk with Jesus's people. This trip has helped me see things I may have missed. Dear, there must be a sermon somewhere here. To live in the present and have interaction with individuals in the here and now."

Darlene chimed in, "Luke, Jesus opens eyes. Now I am going to close mine."

Darlene was in deep sleep when I nudged her and said, "Wake up. Dear, we are ten minutes out of Pittsburg."

Angelia, Kate, and Natalie were home when we returned. I think we had never hugged and kissed each other so long and intently before. Kate wept. We unpacked and gave each the gold necklaces purchased in Bethlehem. Reflective thoughts came to me: "Live in the present. Must we part for a week or even by death to appreciate hugs and kisses for those around us every day?"

Sunday's sermon was already partly formulated: "Places to meet the living Christ."

When Bill stopped in for a visit to welcome us back, he added, "Luke, I am pleased to inform you both church services went well. Attendance was good. Little Mary sang a solo. We need to get her to sing often."

Darlene could not resist: "Luke, did you hear that? The church did well without you trying to prop it up."

"Okay Dear, though I get your point. I must check with the secretary soon. There will be a lot of catching up to do. Please excuse me. I will see you a little later."

"Luke, why are you home from the office so quickly?"

"Darlene, the DS called and asked if I would take a new appointment the cabinet has in mind for me. They would like for me to take Oslow Memorial United Methodist Church."

"No Luke, I am happy here. The girls like school. I like my part-time position at the hospital. So what did you tell him?"

"Dear, I said I may be interested."

"Luke, tell me about Oslow. I don't like the idea. But tell me more."

"Darlene, Oslow has recently moved to a new location where they built a $3 1/2-million church. He said it is absolutely beautiful. He wants us to keep it moving and, of course, help meet the heavy financial challenge. The old church and parsonage are up for sale."

"Heavens! Another parsonage situation?"

"No, they have a new parsonage. We have time. Let us jump in the car and go take a look at it. Let us just do it. As we drive, try to think of it this way: the school is near. Angelia and Kate will be off to college soon. It is a good opportunity for both of us to grow. The church here is well-grounded and growing. Let us be open minded, please."

A couple months later, the church had a going-away party. It turned out to be a thank you and a roasting *get-even-with-him time*. Members made up as many stories about us as they could.

They laughed. I blushed. My minister fishing friend came forward with a gift.

"Luke, I present this gift to help you remember your ministry here and our good fishing days."

"Curley Hurley, what in the world is this? A paddle?"

"This says, 'Don't get caught up the river again without a paddle.'"

Foster Rine stood, "Rev. Hurley, would you kindly explain what the paddle means and what Luke has been doing when he says he visits all day?"

"Gladly, Luke sent me up the lake in a small aluminum johnboat (more like a tin can) while he went back home for the electric motor he forgot. The tin can went this way and then another way until I wore blisters on my hands. He didn't like the low ground where I pitched the tent.

"While fishing, a mean storm came up. We took cover under tall oak trees and several aluminum boats piled on top of each other for shelter. The rain turned into hail the size of golf balls. They banged, popped, bounced into our faces. Everything was so different and frightening. We laughed and giggled like small kids. I will have good memories of you, pal."

After the crowd applauded, Foster said, "We had better warn Oslow church where you like to visit."

A few days later, Jay Henry joined Darlene and me for dinner on the first evening of annual conference. He was quick to share his past few years. "Luke, a couple years ago, the bishop sent me to a disastrous situation. You once spoke of *an-againster* in every church. I did not have one. That church had a hornet's nest full. The senior minister and entire staff stayed in the church. Nothing about me or my sermons were satisfactory for the old timers.

"One dignified leader voiced his dislike for me because of my looks. He said I was just plain ugly. One thing I will say for the bishop. He came and tried to establish some reason but to no avail. In a couple months, he gave me another appointment.

"Since then, all has gone well. As much as he tried to help, I still believe bishops should have limited tenure. They have too much power and for too long. Let them serve a church for a few years in case they have forgotten what it is like down in the trenches. Please don't quote me."

"Jay, it is between you and me. You are not alone in those feelings. Darlene and I are happy for you now. When you are happy, we are happy. Regardless of our circumstances, as John Wesley said, 'Preach Christ.' We will not forget who we are and to whom we belong. We still preach Christ. We love you."

Sometimes later, Oslow Memorial congregation welcomed our family with open arms.

"Darlene, things I had already heard are true. Oslow church is blessed with a large variety of effective ministries. Their music ministry for one is widely known for quality. What more could Christ or congregation do or be? I have a first sermon in mind based on St. Mark 11:1–6. It is powerful and pleasant."

"Luke, please be careful. First impressions are important."

"Dear, I will be kind and pleasant. At least I will try. First, I will acknowledge the congregation for their vision, dedication, and hard work. When it was reported what wonderful miracles Jesus performed, Jesus did not stop. He moved on. His work was not finished. Neither is ours. We can let Christ lead us deeper and wider."

"Dear, please be careful."

"We need to know the members. In our first planning session, I will suggest small neighborhood groups. That could be a good way to become acquainted. You would enjoy it."

"Luke, I plan to seek a job at the hospital and maybe the county health department. College tuitions will be facing us soon."

"Dear, please wait a few weeks. We just got here. After the eleven o'clock service, Syd, the trustee chair, asked us to join him and a few others for lunch after the worship service."

As we drove to the cafeteria, Darlene was inquisitive as usual. "Luke, were you satisfied with the worship service?'

"Dear, basically, yes. The people are friendly. The choir was exceptional."

"Luke, and your sermon?"

"I knew you would ask. Sweetheart, it was okay. It was biblical and relative to their situation. Quite a few people were complimentary. Accolades are always welcomed, but down deep, I know when I communicate or miss the mark. The next sermon may be better and more interesting."

Syd and several others discussed the church debt as we ate lunch. "Luke, I hope you plan to attend our trustees' meeting tonight?"

"Syd, I plan to be there. What is the topic?"

"Reverend, it will be our stressful mortgage payments. A bank rep may show up. They are concerned. We have asked McCorkel, our building contractor, to come. His company is nearly bankrupt. He will be pressing us to pay soon. Reverend, bring your prayers tonight. We will need them."

"Syd, God is with us."

The next night, at 7:05 pm, Syd asked for a prayer. He proceeded to explain our delinquent payments. Jack asked: "Can we claim Chapter 13 or Chapter 11?" A couple laughed.

Syd did not laugh. "Jack, I don't think we should even consider that idea. Mr. McCorkel, can you give us a little more time?"

"Syd, I have been worried about your situation and my personal debts for a long time. It has not been easy, but here is my proposition: If your people could come up with $200,000, I will forget the other $300.000. That is the best I can do. Let me know soon."

After McCorkel left, several trustees promised $10,000 each and expressed interest in contacting others. That night, Darlene was interested to know about the meeting.

"Darlene, God was indeed with us. It was touchy for a while. Call it luck, call it a miracle, or call it willpower, but the problem was solved for a little while. McCorkel virtually ended up excusing the church for $300,000. I believe in unexpected situations. I also believe in miracles."

"Luke, I hear the girls coming in."

"I want to talk with them. Angelia, Kate, how did youth meeting go?"

"Dad, I am too old for that group. One more year, and I will be off to college. It is nothing like we have had before. I don't think Nattie is very experienced working with youth. She doesn't seem to know what to do. We only had eight girls and one boy."

"Angelia, let us be patient. People are still on summer vacation. I have an idea, and I need your help. Why not have a church sleepover soon? We can get them ready for fall activities. Planning sessions we had in the past usually brought surprising results.

"You can drop a few ideas like a bowling party and a ski trip. The kids will have some good ideas. You get me the names and addresses, and I will have secretary Roxie send out a mailing. You two can help her. Better yet, I will ask our associate Will to help Nattie for a few weeks."

Darlene interrupted, "Girls, I will help some, but don't forget I work five days a week at the county health department. And Luke, I will not be able to help with the wedding this weekend. Sorry."

"But, Dear, this is a big wedding. The college president and many notables will be there."

"Sorry again, I will be at a health department workshop. You girls are on your own."

The wedding rehearsal went well without Darlene there to help. I gave my usual speech, "Only children ages five and older are to participate. Attention is on the bride and groom. In the excitement of rehearsal and wedding, please be careful driving tonight and tomorrow. Come early for the wedding. We want it to run smoothly. I thank the parents. They love you and have brought you to this grand moment. We pray."

Sunday afternoon, Darlene was pleased to tell of the enjoyment of her workshop. Then she asked about the wedding. Angelia and Kate wanted to explain since they were there and also at the dinners. I insisted on telling the eventful evening myself.

"Darlene, I have never been more embarrassed for a wedding. First of all, the ushers were thirty minutes late. The organist started the wedding processional at the proper time. The foot-high carpet roll was in the isle which was supposed to have been unrolled to the altar. The first bridesmaid tried to step over but stopped.

"The bride's father ran down and unrolled the carpet. That was troublesome enough. But during the ceremony, one attendant after the other collapsed. They swaggered, wilted, and fell. After all was said and done, the bride and groom were married. Everyone was happy. They thanked the preacher for being calm through it all. Dear, aren't you surprised I was calm?"

"Yes, I am. But you are not calm now."

A few days later, Monday morning when I walked in the office, Roxie handed me the phone, "Luke, this is the DS."

"Good morning. This is your good friend Ken. Luke, remember the pastor's retreat Thursday? Two areas are all set. I need a third one. I know this is short notice, but would you give a lecture on 'church planning'"?

"Ken, I see you are *planning ahead*. Yes, I would be glad to help. It is my favorite area."

"Luke, please explain what first prompted you to get interested in planning skills?"

"Ken, God gets the credit. Christ put a fire under me. He gave me a new dream for my life. I wanted others to catch the fire. I gathered others together to dream. Once involved, they became engaged. Once engaged, they were motivated to make their dream become a reality. That is the short answer to your question. I am not the only one using a planning method, but I will see you Thursday."

"All right, staff, grab your coffee. Let us do a little planning ourselves."

"Luke, before we start, allow me to ask a question. I saw your Indian point collection the other day when I visited. I would love to go on a hunt with you sometime."

"Will, I would enjoy your company. We will need to plan some Friday morning. I don't like taking off early in the week. On Sunday, we get reports of members in the hospital. First-time visitors need a visit. If no funerals or weddings on the weekend, Friday is our best day."

"Luke, I foresee a problem. We could end up working two or three weeks without a day off."

"Will, you are very insightful. Let us plan on this Friday for an Indian hunt. Now let us talk about church planning. Nattie, how are youth activities going?"

"They are going fine. Angelia talked about a time to plan fall programs. Sounds good to me. Will is willing to help us for a few weeks. With our team, we will get things going. We plan to help Roxie with the newsletter and mailing."

"Thank you for such a fine report. Let us be thinking about some potential new church members. Maybe in the spring, we will start classes. Will, would you call on a couple of our recent worship visitors? I will visit a couple in the hospital and Rob at home. He says he is dying with cancer. Add him to your prayer list. Let us pray."

Later, Rob's voice cracked as he tried to whisper his concerns. "Those are pictures of my family. I will miss them. I love them so much. Reverend, I take comfort and strength in Psalm 139. My God knew me and you and each member of our family while still in our mother's womb. God has been with us through the years and will take care of us into the future."

"Rob, those are helpful words. We will pray and walk with you and your family all the way."

The week was busy and fulfilling. Darlene brought up a subject that I knew was overdue. "Luke, our lives have gotten too busy, even hectic. Why don't we take the girls out for dinner? We can allow them to invite a friend. Friday evening is our designated night out anyway."

"Dear, that is a tremendous idea. Let Angelia and Kate choose the place to eat. We can come back to the house for desert and games. Darlene, you come up with remarkable ideas."

In a free moment, I called Matt. "Matt, we can't go Indian hunting Friday. Darlene reminded me that it is family evening out. We are going to dinner with Angelia and Kate. They will invite a couple friends. We would like for you to join us. Although against my policy to take Monday off, let us meet early Monday morning.

"We will grab a McDonald's biscuit and head for New River. After this week of rain, fields at Crump's Bottom will be perfect. The points will jump out and call our name. We will talk Sunday."

Three days later, the rough dirt road followed the river about 5 mi. to a dead end where we parked the Isuzu Trooper. Walking sticks in hand, we slowly crisscrossed the field with eyes glued to the ground. Will caught on quickly and found his first of several points. At noon, we took a lunch break of

Sardines and mustard. Will asked, "Do you still hunt wild game with your shotgun?"

"Will, I quit a few years ago."

"Why?"

"I was influenced by one of Albert Schweitzer's books. He advocated 'reverence for life.' Besides, I saw my cousin clubbing a raccoon caught in a steel trap. I just became tired of killing innocent animals. I believed they wanted to live, eat, and enjoy their families. Friends have said I kill fish. Yes, I am inconsistent. Let us continue our hunt." After a couple more hours, Will motioned me to stop. "Luke, I don't mind being soaked, but did you remember official board meeting is at seven tonight?"

"Oh, yes, we better get back to the jeep. I sure hope the road out of here is not flooded."

It was. Water covered low places in the road. We stood and looked. "Will, the water is too deep to go forward." Will placed a rock at the water's edge, and in five minutes, it was covered.

"Luke, what are we going to do?"

"Will, we are marooned."

"You mean stuck."

"Yes. Stuck."

"Will, I believe my Isuzu could climb up that steep hill. Let's give it a try. First, we need to fill the ditch with rocks, sticks, logs, or whatever to get the jeep started up the hill. You are strong. Take my pocket knife and try whittling a couple of those small trees enough to pull them down."

Two hours later, I said, "Will, think it is safe up here? If the river gets higher, we will have to get Noah's Ark."

"Luke, obviously, we can't follow the road. What now?"

"Will, we must climb the hill and hope there is a main road up there somewhere."

"Hill, heck, it is a mountain!"

After a steady climb, we found a fruit tree with a couple gnarled, rough, pitted apples. After dark, we hit an old logging road which eventually led us to an old log cabin. Drenched and dirty, we knocked. An elderly woman opened and invited us in. "My name is Jennie. I don't see people very often. Come on in. I will get you a cup of hot coffee and a slice of my cornbread."

Will explained, "We are lost preachers. I mean we got lost down by the river and are trying to find a road to get back home. What is your address?"

"Boys, I don't know. My son brings me groceries about once a week. I call him if I need something. I have never had a preacher visit me before. It means a lot. Thank you for coming."

I called the church and told the chairman: "Will and I are out of town. We are not going to make it to board meeting tonight because of high water. We are fine. Please explain to everyone. See you tomorrow." After a Scripture reading and prayer, I called Angelia to come and look for us.

"Dad, tell me where you are."

"We don't know, except it will be on a ridge road. Please come. Take a right-paved mountain road before you get to the river. We will be waiting and watching for you. Thanks."

When the river went down, Will and I retrieved the Jeep. Of course, Darlene asked, "Did anyone at the church learn the factual circumstances of your river experience?"

"Darling, not as far as I know. But at the Methodist men's meeting, the chairman announced, 'Since Luke enjoys mud, water, rivers, and mountains so much, I am going to invite him

REV. FRANK E. BOURNER

on our Ramp dig next month. Oh, Luke, you may not have heard. A new preacher coming to our church has to be initiated with a Ramp dig and dinner. It is actually a lot of fun. It is our way of saying welcome.' Dear, there was something about the group's response that triggered a note of suspicion. Let's change the subject."

I have had time to think of Sunday's sermon. Recall last Sunday how the disciples reported Jesus's good works. The Scripture continues explaining how Jesus moved on. This Sunday, I explain how the church must keep moving on. I plan to tell my story of corn planting on Uncle Pete's farm."

"That is one story you never told me."

"Good, you will get to hear it Sunday."

"I guess I won't. It is my turn in the nursery. Give me a little sampling if you have time."

"Well, when I was young, Nani sent me to the farm. Uncle Pete sent my two cousins to replant corn where a previous planting failed to germinate. It was a scorching day. We sat under a hickory tree and cracked nuts and laughed. Paul took the entire burlap sack of corn seeds, dug a hole in the middle of the field, and planted them.

"A few weeks later, Uncle Pete visited that field. You can guess the ending of that story. The church must spread the Gospel of Christ, not in one place only but far and wide. It will be a message on outreach based on Mathew 13 scattering the seeds."

"Luke, it sounds a little long. Needs a bit of polishing, but your point will be well taken—hopefully. Our agenda this week is full."

"Yes, my dear. There is staff meeting, newsletter, bulletins, phone calls, drop-in visitors. And, oh, yes, Wednesday night and a sermon."

"Dear, this week will be full and exciting. Jesus promised joy and fulfillment. We sure have plenty of it. Serving the Lord and others is life. I have heard talk about ministerial perks. Joyfully serving the Lord is a big perk. The Apostle Paul said it: 'I am running over with joy' in 2 Corinthians 7:4."

"Luke, when that mind of yours starts rolling, it seldom stops. Now go to the church and get the joy."

The joy was staff meeting, newsletter, bulletin info, phone calls, sermon, and Wednesday night lecture refinement; and the phone rang.

"Luke, this is Moody. You remember Thursday, we leave for the Ramp dig. I will accompany you in your Jeep. The guys think your Jeep will come in handy in the mud and snow. Besides, you will need to be back for Sunday service. Pick me up at the church at 2:00 p.m. Thursday."

A couple days later, it was a two-hour drive to their mountain cabin. Friday morning, after bacon, eggs, biscuits, and gravy, we jumped in the Jeep and were off to somewhere.

"Moody, I have no idea where we are going or what we are going to do."

"Luke, hang tight. The road will be rough with a few inches of snow and ice."

With the hearty breakfast, shovels, burlap sacks, and knives, I thought this must be a very special and secret mission. It must be secret because I had not seen another vehicle or human for over an hour. Soon, the guys were scrapping snow away as if looking for a hidden treasure. Walter called, "I found some up here." I hurried up to see the prize.

"Those are weeds you have been looking for?"

"No. Ramps!"

"What are they for?" I asked.

"'Here, eat one," he answered.

"No, thanks. They smell like onions but worse."

"Luke, just wait until we clean the mud off, take them to the church, cut them up, and prepare them for a big Ramp dinner next Saturday. People travel for miles for our annual feast."

I thought but did not say, *They won't need a map. They will be able to smell the repugnant odor several counties away.*

Late Saturday afternoon, I was pleased to leave camp mud for home. The guys gave me a cheerful send off with a promise to clean the mud off my Jeep next week.

After a few miles, a terrible smell found my nostrils. The farther I drove, the more repugnant it became. "Did I run over a skunk?" I asked myself.

After washing mud and grit from the vehicle, I decided to pull the rubber floor mats and spray them. There in front of my eyes, I mean nose, was the repugnant culprit—several stems of smashed Ramps. For a moment, I could see my good Christian friends back at the cabin laughing.

The district pastors' retreat began on Thursday afternoon. After handing out helpful materials and outlines, I explained at some length skills and methods of group planning. I tried to communicate the joy of watching their group become excited about their dreams and, later, the realized results. The two lectures seemed well received. After the session, Alex approached. "Luke, after all a pastor has to do in a week, I think your plan expects too much. I am not a multitasker. I am not a juggler. If I try to keep five eggs in the air at one time, I will drop one or more and make a complete mess."

"Wait a minute, Alex. You are a man with a number of talents. All Christ asks of us is to use the talents we have."

"Thank you, but I am not a juggler."

Before departing, Ken asked me to step in a side room. He thanked me for my contribution to the retreat. He said he presented me to the cabinet for a district superintendent position and asked my opinion and continued: "Luke, I would like to hear more about your Christmas Eve worship service. It sounds interesting."

"Oh, no. The chairperson called you Ken? In short, it was not very worshipful. The youth director insisted on having a live lamb that night. She placed it on a table with four poles, a string for the fence and a little straw. My sermon theme was 'Silent Night, Holy Night,' but it turned out not to be silent nor holy.

"The little shepherd boy turned to his mother two rows back and screamed, 'Mom, it's peeing.' The lamb's legs skid first one way and the other until it fell off the table and ran with ushers chasing."

"Luke, that is funny. After all, the Son of God was born in a cattle stall. I have your back. If you don't mind, I would like to preach for you this Sunday. Peace."

When I arrived home, I found Darlene exhausted. "Dear, are you feeling well?"

"Not really. Life at the health department has been stressful lately. I have missed you. The girls are starting to get things together for college. You have been gone a lot. You know I have welcomed your time with the boys' Ramp hunting and your lecture with the district pastors, but I miss you. I have been tired a great deal. Dr. Blazing informed me that my heart was not functioning properly. I go back next week. I need you more than ever."

"I am so sorry. Glad you saw the doctor and going back for a follow-up. I need to be more helpful. Help me through our next evangelism program. After that, we need to find time to consider retirement. I often dream about us having a house of our own. We can financially do it.

"Stay healthy, so we can think about our own house and time to travel. Ken expressed appreciation for my lecture and offered to preach for me this Sunday. That will give us a free time to consider retirement. I love you so much."

"Luke, please tell me more about this new evangelism program."

"Our committee has invited Dr. Eddie Fox and Dr. George Morris to lead us in a city-wide crusade. George asked me join them in Tonga for a South East clergy-lay week of teaching. I declined."

"Luke, I read articles about the crusade in our newspaper."

"Yes, plans are, well, in progress."

"Luke, did you see today's newspaper? Not everyone is pleased about your crusade. Here it is. Listen: 'The fundamental pastor's fellowship tells Christians not to attend. The crusade is evil. They don't believe God's Word. They preach salvation by good works. They are false teachers. Don't attend.'"

"That is sad, terrible, but it won't stop us. Their resistance may even help. Attendance will be good."

Ken kept his promise. He preached a faith-centered sermon on Paul's conversion. He emphasized how God and Ananias cured his blindness. Paul's eyes were opened wide, very wide. He talked about new life in Christ. As he preached, I thought, *God opened my eyes years ago to wonders unimaginable. How many scales do I still have? Open my eyes wider. What spiritual gifts have I been missing? Your Word says you have countless blessings for those who love you. Countless…*

After the service, we took him to dinner. Darlene whispered, "You and Ken go alone. I am exhausted. I don't feel well."

"Darlene, please come along. We are going to your favorite restaurant. I will not let it linger too long. This afternoon, we will take a good rest."

As usual, the dinner and service were excellent. Conversation centered on the children.

"Tell me about the girls," he asked.

Darlene was slow to answer. I waited for her involvement. "Ken, Rachael is attending WVU and majoring in education. Kate is a student at WV Wesleyan. We miss them dearly, but they are both happy."

The rest of the day was quiet. Darlene mostly slept. The next morning, she was slow getting up which was unusual for her.

"Dear, why don't you stay home today? The health department will get along one day without you. Let's both take the day off."

"Luke, you know I can't do that. Maybe I will come home early."

By midday, the phone rang: "Luke, this is Dixie at the clinic. Darlene fainted and has been taken to St. Luke's Hospital. Come, I will meet you there."

The wait was long and painful. When Dr. Blazing came to meet us, he was slow to speak. "We could not revive her. I am so sorry. She had a massive heart attack. There was nothing we could do."

With those words and the finality of her death, something within me died for two years. Two years later, when Brian visited, he said, "Luke, you are looking much better. How have you coped?"

"Brian, I have suffered two years of pain, loneliness, even anger. I had dreams of being trapped, being in a deep valley where I could not climb out. There was no one with a hand to lift me over the top. Brian, Murphy's Law is something like this, 'When things go wrong, they will get worse.' I now know why friends say, 'Don't make important decisions for two years.' I made a few wrong ones. God, please forgive me."

"Brian, I am talking too much."

"Luke, please go on. I will benefit from your journey. Please…"

"I feel much better now. That old sermon Darlene said she liked very much came back to me. It was 'Ground Zero and Lift Off.' My ground zero is Christ. Christ lifted me. He lifted me through the years. Christ gave me life, and He still does. Brian, our mind is only so large. I came to realize that if I dwell on negatives, resentment, troubles, it would only pull me deeper into that awful valley.

"The way to crowd those things out was for me to fill my mind with ground zero, Christ. My first compulsion was to serve and witness Christ. That is where I am now, and that is where I am headed. That was my calling, and that is still my purpose. The Divine Potter is still working with this old lump of clay to accomplish His purpose.

"Luke will continue to preach Christ. I want to tell everyone to make the most out of this one life they have on earth. Bible study, fellowship, and prayer is the way. 'I will press on toward the mark of the high calling of God in Christ Jesus.' Thank you for listening.

"Brian, when this earthly journey is over, I will go to the home where Jesus, Yvonne, Rev. Shepherd, Nan Goodwin, Francis Asbury, and countless other faithful servants are enjoying that which 'eye hast not seen nor ear heard the wonderful things waiting for those who love the Lord.'"

> Wherefore seeing we also are compassed about with so great a cloud of witnesses, let us lay aside every weight, and the sin which doth so easily beset us, and let us run with patience the race that is set before us, Looking unto Jesus the author and finisher of our faith; who for the joy that was set before him endured the cross, despising the shame, and is set down at the right hand of the throne of God. (Hebrews 12:1–2)

> Behold, I shew you a mystery; we shall not all sleep, but we shall all be changed, In a moment, in the twinkling of an eye, at the last trump: for the trumpet shall sound, and the dead shall be raised incorruptible, and we shall be changed.

For this corruptible must put on incorruption, and this mortal must put on immortality.

So when this corruptible shall have put on incorruption, and this mortal shall have put on immortality, then shall be brought to pass the saying that is written, Death is swallowed up in victory.

O death, where is thy sting? O grave, where is thy victory? The sting of death is sin; and the strength of sin is the law. But thanks be to God, which gives us the victory through our Lord Jesus Christ.

Therefore, my beloved brethren, be ye steadfast, unmovable, always abounding in the work of the Lord, forasmuch as ye know that your labor is not in vain in the Lord. (1 Corinthians 15:51–58, King James Version)

The Good Shepherd seeks those who stray. (An allegory)

One wooly ewe wandered in the desert hill country. She was far from her shepherd, her stockade, protection, and community of friends. Food and water were scarce. Dangers lurked. Nighttime shadows stole her sleep. Breezes swirled first in one direction and then another like a voice with contradicting advice: "Turn homeward," the wind whispered.

"No! I can't! Go find another flock and another shepherd or learn to live alone."

Deep into that disturbing night, she pondered causes for her eerie plight. Answers drifted through, slowly at first, followed by a sandstorm of reasons or excuses. "My shepherd favored the younger, attractive, aggressive ewe recently brought into the fold. His favoritism was obvious. My performance and occasional questions were ignored or rebuked. I was older, more experienced, and more talented than that new one to his fold.

"I had served faithfully for twenty-five years. Did I not deserve more favorable treatment? The flock quickly distanced itself from me. That hurt. The flock, by nature, would respond to the desire of their shepherd. I could not blame them, or maybe I should.

"They had been my friends. Maybe I simply imagined their ill-will when nothing personal was intended. Even if I decide to return, I have no idea which direction is home."

When my storm of anger subsided and a soft breeze returned, I wondered what thoughts were going through the shepherd's head. In fact, the shepherd did have sleepless nights considering his senseless ewe. *That foolish, spiritually sick, jealous ewe deserves the desert*, he thought. *I will ignore her. I have a flock. I am the shepherd. I am the boss. I will choose a greener course and leave the lost one behind. Let her be a lesson to the others. Maybe she will come to her senses and meekly return to the fold.*

Then a fresh, discomforting thought blazed through his head like a comet in the night: "What would the Good Shepherd do?"

The answer was disquieting but compelling. "Without thoughts of why the sheep went astray, the Good Shepherd would secure his fold, hurry out in search, find the lost ewe, tenderly wrap the wounded one in his arms, and turn toward security of home." Sufficiently prompted, he laid aside his vindictive spirit. He left the cozy fold to search for his ewe somewhere on a hill far away.

Appendix

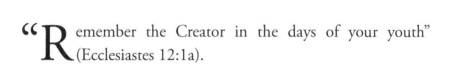

"Remember the Creator in the days of your youth" (Ecclesiastes 12:1a).

Profound truth in this writer's words: "The explosive power of a new affection" (Dr. Thomas Carlyle, 1796–1881).

My home was not Christian. It was filled with skepticism. A minister visited my dad at the coal company where he worked. He told my father he was responsible for his children's attendance in church. When my father came home, he announced, "Get ready. We are going to church tonight! At the altar call, my father went forward, knelt, and wept. Mother joined him. Dad stood up and came straight to me. He put his arms around me and whispered, 'I have found something tonight that I wanted and I want you to have.' That night, I gave my life to God. After that, I experienced great joy. I wanted to hug everyone. Later I said I wanted to become a preacher. (Rev. Dr. George Morris)

My father was an ordained minister in the Nazarene church. I was in the church three times a week. When I was three years of age, my dad explained how Jesus died for our sins, was crucified, and rose again. He asked me if I understood and if I would invite Jesus into my heart to live with me forever. I said yes. Jesus came into my heart and is with me to this day. (Shirley Hutchison)

"Like Father, Like Son," a song written by Paul Overstreet and Don Schlitz sung by artist Lionel Cartwright, 1989. Also, "Like Father and Mother like Daughter Is a Truth."

"Therefore if any man be in Christ, he is a new creature: old things are passed away; behold, all things are become new" (2 Corinthians 5: 17).

And if it seem evil unto you to serve the LORD, choose you this day whom ye will serve; whether the gods which your fathers served that were on the other side of the flood, or the gods of the Amorites, in whose land ye dwell: but as for me and my house, we will serve the LORD. (Joshua 24:15)

When I consider thy heavens, the work of
thy fingers, the moon and the stars, which
thou hast ordained; What is man, that thou
art mindful of him? and the son of man, that
thou visitest him? For thou hast made him a
little lower than the angels, and hast crowned
him with glory and honour. (Psalms 8:3–5)

Recall Elijah's experience. He retreated to a cave in fear.
There was wind, earthquake, and fire but only in quietness did
he hear God's voice and direction (1 Kings 19:12).

Moses retreated to the mountain and later came down with
the Ten Commandments.

Jesus went to the desert or wilderness for forty days and
nights where he heard direction for ministry (Matthew 4:11).
He also retreated to a quiet place in the Garden of Gethsemane.
There, he received strength to proceed to Jerusalem.

Sometimes it is not the roses but the thorns;
Not the bright city lights but a sleepless night;
In the darkness we see the stars;
And hear God whisper. (FEB)

"In quietness and confidence, you shall find your strength"
(Isaiah 30:15).

Jesus is calling for us to open the door wide. "Behold, I
stand at the door, and knock: if any man hear my voice, and
open the door, I will come in to him, and will sup with him,
and he with me" (Revelation 3:20).

God says He has good plans for us. Good things for which we hoped (Jeremiah 29:11).

Spring Song
FEB

(Dedicated to my faithful wife of fifty-six years)
The hills are asleep like peace in winter.
Trees sparkle with ice like silver rivers.
Streams creep along very slow.
Life's buried under blankets of snow.
The hills are asleep like peace in winter.
Waiting for springtime.
The warm kiss of sunshine.
To awaken the prince of nature's mind.
Spring is a special time.
Cascading brooks beat a theme.
The sun has a friendly beam.
Boys and girls like to dream.
Young hearts learn to sing.
Seeds sprout up through warming soil.
Put forth flowers of colors royal.
Lovers walk hand in hand.
Give and take wedding bands.
I like spring through and through.
But in every season, I love you.

"George and I have been happily married for sixty-three years, and because we are Christians, we have always put our own desires last and have been thoughtful of desires of the other spouse" (Mrs. Barbara Morris).

Memories
FEB

I would like my memories for years to come,
Be a mind full of pleasant ones,
To leave a nostalgic trail,
Winding joyfully through the vale,
Of happy days, funny things,
Laughter and tall tales,
Of rest, love, and peace at setting sun,
I want the days and years of pain,
To be no more than a gentle rain,
Soil prepared for flowers of spring,
Love, togetherness it does bring—
Though a physical sigh, a spiritual gain,
The deepest satisfaction, the devotion of my wife,
Who shares her love these years of my life,
With children and grandchildren as well,
To crown our years with the richer wealth.

"But the fruit of the Spirit is love, joy, peace, longsuffering, gentleness, goodness, faith, meekness, temperance: against such there is no law" (Galatians 5:22–23).

Later that day, I shared a dream I had last night.
"Darlene, I had a dream about delegating responsibility."
"Luke, please tell me your dream."

"Darlene, there were two characters. I was both of them, Corporate and Luke. Corporate said, 'Delegate. Get others to do the task.'

"Luke responded, 'Delegate and, at the same time, be personally involved in troubled lives of others.'

"Corporate answered: 'I like directing others. Involvement consumes. It takes away from my pleasures. Being involved can be messy.'

"Luke tried to explain his position, 'We are followers of Jesus. He delegated and he also mixed with crowds at the same time. He wept, He touched, and bled. He told the power of God to save. He was the Good Shepherd.'"

Darlene, as was her nature, put the issue back to her dear husband, "Luke, did you make a decision for yourself?"

"No, Dear, I suppose the debate goes on."

God's Creation
FEB

Bird gliding low to alight,
And I, I ask myself,
In heaven's name, what right,
Have I to take its life,
To stop its heart from beating?
Life was not mine to give,
And it is not mine to take,
But it is for me to muse,
Praise and celebrate God's creation.

God's Creation 2
FEB

Ever see manmade lights on the street?
Beautiful as God's lightening streak;
Animals in a cage, however sleek;
Lovely as raccoons playing in a creek;
Or a painted bird on the page;
Lovely as a sparrow in the sage?

Heaven Is Near
FEB

Heaven—how could Thee improve on this?
Firmament, the mountains tenderly kiss.
Clouds slowly drifting by.
They have no worries; they own the sky.
Heaven—how could Thee improve on this?
River meanders in tranquil bliss.
Earth adorned in luscious green.
Heaven could not improve a thing.
Take your time to sit very still.
Heaven is near; heaven is real.

Retirement
FEB

Time passes quickly.
I was a crawling child,
A running boy,

A driven man.
Speed faster, my soul.
Reach for the sky,
It's my time to fly,
Could this soul ever slow,
Or even stop?
Father time knows.

Doug was director of developmental disabilities. He had a compassionate concern for persons with special needs. He had requested the old-fashioned petunia as flowers for his funeral. I was asked to incorporate his request in my remarks.

The Old Fashioned Petunia
FEB

Old fashioned petunias grew beside our house
    when I was a boy.
"They've been around forever," the older folk
    said.
After years of showing forth bell-shaped glory,
their bright colors faded into pale blue, pink,
    and white.
Without fail, they reappeared year after year
    to catch
my eye and fascinate my young mind.
While petunias grew in ancient times,
they and their cousins still persist, namely
    potatoes,

tobacco, jimson, eggplant, tomatoes, and
    chili peppers.
But most of all, my heart belongs to the
    old-fashioned petunia.
And now as a man, my pensive mind slips
    back
to that old-fashioned flower.
Faded—yes,
Common—true,
Unnoticed—usually,
Trampled upon—often,
Much like humans on the street every day.
Look deeply into their faded faces.
See the fainting, struggling people all around—
Ignored,
Trampled upon,
Waiting for my eye,
Waiting for my ear,
Waiting for my time,
Waiting for my touch,
Waiting for my love,
Waiting for a cup of water like the Master
    said,
"As you give to them, you give to me."
Look deeply into the faded bell-shaped bloom.
Look deeply to see the beauty.
Look deeply to see the promise.
Look deeply—and see God.

Possible Discussion Questions

1. What do you think of Isaiah's statement that God is the potter and we are the clay? How about Isaiah: 64:8 and Jeremiah 29:11?
2. When did you first believe deeply in Jesus Christ and the resurrection?
3. In what ways have you grown as a Christian?
4. How do you witness for Jesus Christ? Name a Christian who best demonstrates strong verbal witness.
5. How important is church attendance?
6. What do you look for or expect in a church?
7. In what ways would you like to grow as a Christian?

About the Author

Rev. Frank E. Bourner was a United Methodist pastor in West Virginia for thirty-six years and interim pastor in several North Carolina charges after retirement. He earned an AB from Marshall College in religion and philosophy and his divinity degree from Duke Divinity School.

CPSIA information can be obtained
at www.ICGtesting.com
Printed in the USA
BVHW031920260820
587409BV00001B/331